"You're Out Of Your Depth," Brody Said Softly.

Caitlyn managed to smile. "I'm not worried. I can take care of—"

"Yourself. I know." She was such a reckless little girl, he thought.

His attraction to her was an irresistible force. She had touched a place inside of him that was desperately needy, and he wanted more.

Ironically, she was so innocent and trusting, his conscience prodded him to improve her odds against him. "You don't want to play this game with me," he said. "I'm not sure how experienced you are, and I'm likely to cheat."

Caitlyn drew a breath, and when she spoke, the words came too fast. "I'm not playing games. I don't know what you're talking about."

"Don't you?"

"No."

Brody's voice dropped to a silky drawl. "Then would you like a demonstration?"

Dear Reader,

Happy summertime reading from all of us here at Silhouette! As the days of summer wind to an end, take the time to curl up with August's wonderful love stories. These are books as hot as the most sizzling summer's day!

We start with Mary Lynn Baxter's *Man of the Month* novel *Tall in the Saddle,* which has a hero you'll never forget—Flint Carson, a man as rugged and untamed as the land he ranches. This is a book you'll want to read over and over again. It's a keeper!

Also in August comes a wild, witty romp from Lass Small, *The Molly Q.* Don't ask me to explain; I'll just say it has to do with computers, kidnapping and marvelous fun.

Rounding out August is *A Wolf in Sheep's Clothing,* a tie-in to July's *Never Tease a Wolf*—both by the talented Joan Johnston. And don't miss books from Naomi Horton, Ryanne Corey and Sally Goldenbaum. Each and every Silhouette Desire novel this month is one that I am keeping in my personal library.

So go wild with Desire—you'll be glad you did.

All the best,

Lucia Macro
Senior Editor

RYANNE COREY

LEATHER AND LACE

SILHOUETTE Desire®

Published by Silhouette Books New York

America's Publisher of Contemporary Romance

SILHOUETTE BOOKS
300 East 42nd St., New York, N.Y. 10017

LEATHER AND LACE

ISBN: 0-373-05657-5

First Silhouette Books printing August 1991

Printed in the U.S.A.

Books by Ryanne Corey

Silhouette Desire

The Valentine Street Hustle #615
Leather and Lace #657

RYANNE COREY

loves to travel, but for the first few years of her marriage, the majority of her travel experiences consisted of trips to and from the hospital to have her children. Four boys and one girl later, she decided to broaden her horizons. Unfortunately, it seemed wherever she and her husband traveled, disaster followed. A trip to Mexico coincided with a hurricane. When they visited Hawaii, a volcano erupted. And, yes, they visited San Francisco just before the earthquake.

Luckily, Ryanne has a good sense of humor. She says, "Life is entirely too serious to be taken seriously." And by far, the most important ingredient in her work is humor.

One

There were only two good reasons to spend time in Ticaboo, Arizona: the venison pot roast at Bird's Café and the pretty red-haired waitress named Isabelle who served the venison pot roast. Brody Walker was a big fan of both, and he checked into his room at the rundown Ticaboo Tourist Lodge with a smile on his face. Everything was just as he remembered it—the lock was missing from the door, there was no TV, and the light globe hanging from a chain in the middle of the ceiling had burned out. No, he definitely didn't stay in Ticaboo for the luxurious accommodations. He could have driven another couple of hours and stayed in Page where the motel room came with locks and light globes, but he was a man who had his priorities in order. A good meal and the company of a warm-hearted woman more than made up for a night at the Ticaboo Tourist Lodge.

He showered in lukewarm water, then dressed in clean jeans and a denim shirt. The light above the bathroom mirror flickered on and off like a neon sign, but he managed to shave without skinning himself alive. However, pulling on his cowboy boots was a major and painful undertaking. He'd cracked a couple of ribs at the Frontier Days Rodeo in Pinetop, thanks to a mean-tempered bronco who had danced a jig on his chest. Fortunately, sweet Isabelle had a notorious soft spot for battered cowboys.

It was nearly ten o'clock when he walked across the road to Bird's Café. The night air smelled of rain, though the temperature was still well above eighty. Brody looked up and down the street, smiling at this sleepy wisp of a town buried in moth-eaten pines. One traffic light blinked a lazy, permanent yellow. The drugstore, the sheriff's office and the supermarket were interspersed with vacant lots overgrown with weeds. The muffled thump of a bass guitar could be heard from the roadhouse down the street. A pickup truck with a shaggy collie in the back rambled past at a sedate ten miles an hour. Brody noticed that the driver stopped at the deserted intersection for a full minute before proceeding. Such was Ticaboo.

A faded sign in the window of the café advertised world-famous paprika potato logs. Another sign offered night crawlers at a dollar a dozen. Brody pushed the door open with the heel of his hand, grinning as he spotted the pretty redhead standing behind the counter. Isabelle's hair had grown to shoulder length since he'd seen her last fall, a wild mane of miniature corkscrew curls.

"Why, Miss Izzy B," Brody drawled in his best John Wayne imitation, "you've done gone and permed your hair."

"Brody?" Isabelle slapped her hands on her cheeks, her eyes growing wide. "Brody Walker! I don't believe it."

"Believe it," Brody said, holding his arms open. He regretted the gesture as soon as Isabelle raced around the counter and grabbed him in a bone-crushing hug. His bones were already crushed. "That's real nice," he gasped, patting Isabelle on her permed head. "It's good to see you, Izzy. I drove fifty miles out of my way just to—ouch!"

"What is it?" Isabelle pulled back, looking at him with a stricken expression. "Oh, Brody, what have you done this time?"

"Well . . . it's my ribs," Brody said, trying to look needy.

"You broke your ribs?"

"Not all of them." He sighed deeply. "Just two. Actually I was pretty lucky, considering the fall I took. It could have been a lot worse."

Isabelle went into action like the seasoned professional she was—so to speak. She helped Brody to a table by the window, then brought him his favorite meal: venison pot roast with mushroom gravy, mashed potatoes and corn on the cob. In between waiting on customers she sympathized while he described his painful encounter with a horse named Cross-Eyed Sue. To cheer him up, she told a few shady jokes she had heard from truck drivers passing through. Isabelle was a peach, a down-home woman who enjoyed sharing a good hearty laugh. Brody liked women he could laugh with, particularly when they were well-endowed and tremendously compassionate.

"So when do you get off?" Brody asked, finishing off the last bite of pecan pie.

"Same as always. Whenever the last customer leaves." Isabelle glanced at the watch on her wrist. "Another hour or so. How long are you in town?"

"I have to be in Moab day after tomorrow. I'm riding in the Canyonlands Rodeo."

Isabelle pursed her lips and cocked one thinly plucked brow. "That doesn't give us much time to get reacquainted, does it?"

"No, it sure doesn't," Brody said regretfully. "I'd offer to take you dancing over at the roadhouse, but my poor ribs . . ."

"There's all kinds of dancing, Brody Walker," she replied with an ingenuous smile. "I suppose you're staying at the lodge?"

"This is Ticaboo, angel. It was either there or the back of my truck."

Isabelle stood, tossing her curly red hair. "I don't think the back of your truck would be very comfortable, do you?"

Brody propped his elbow on the table and his chin in his hand. "Not for dancing," he drawled softly, deep creases framing his slow smile. "And I do love the way you dance."

"You blue-eyed devil." Isabelle giggled, rumpling his dark gold hair. "Why you keep riding the rodeo circuit, I'll never know. One of these days you're going to do yourself some permanent damage, and what a sin and a shame that would be."

Brody shifted uncomfortably on his chair. "Your concern is touching."

"Living dangerously is a foolish pastime," Isabelle went on, pointing a purple painted fingernail at him. "A heartbreaker like yourself has an obligation to womankind, Brody Walker. Why don't you stop wrestling with broncos and Brahma bulls and concentrate on running that ranch of yours in Wyoming? I hear it's a real showplace."

"Guess I'm just one of those bowlegged, bull-doggin' cowboys at heart, ma'am."

Isabelle rolled her eyes at his country bumpkin act. "No one can shovel manure quite like you do, Brody."

"Thank you."

"But it's still manure. I do wish you would find yourself a nice hobby that wouldn't endanger your vital parts."

Brody tipped his chair back on two legs and smiled lazily at her. "Not to worry, Izzy B, my vital parts are hanging in there. And speaking of which, I'm in number six over at the lodge. How about we meet there in an hour?"

Isabelle grinned, gave his shoulder a squeeze and went to work. Brody finished off his coffee, then blew a kiss to Isabelle and walked outside. The wind had picked up and thunder rolled over the pines. It wouldn't be long before the sky opened up in a full-blown storm. He quickened his pace, heading to the roadhouse. The music was so loud he couldn't tell if it was bad or good, but the foot-stomping rhythm was catching. He grabbed a seat at the bar, tossed down a couple of drinks and watched the clock through a blanket of low-hanging smoke. When he walked outside at ten to twelve, the rain was falling in earnest, thrashing the scrubby pines and packing weeds flat. He ran through the cloud of vapor rising from the warm asphalt road, feeling raindrops pepper the back of his neck. It was a scene he'd played often in the past few years, killing time in a sleepy town while the sky rained down on him. He felt almost at home.

By the time he reached his room, his shirt was plastered to his back and his hair was dripping in his eyes. He fumbled in his pocket for the key, then recalled he was staying in the Ticaboo Taj Mahal. Keys were not necessary.

He walked into the room and automatically flipped the light switch. The room remained stubbornly dark, and he remembered the burned-out globe. "So what do you expect for sixteen bucks a night, Walker?" Brody asked himself logically, feeling his way to the vinyl chair just inside the door. He sat down and tugged off his sodden boots, another exercise in masochism. His side was killing him. The bandage supporting his injured ribs was just as wet and limp as his shirt, so he stripped it off along with everything else. He was generally miserable from head to foot, and just for a minute entertained the notion that he might be lonely, as well. But only for a moment. Sweet Isabelle would soon arrive, and Brody would have all the comfort and attention a weary traveler could ask for.

He went to the bathroom and rubbed the moisture from his skin and hair, then wrapped the towel around his waist and splashed on a little Old Spice. Izzy B liked Old Spice. He finger-combed his hair, then took a quick look at himself in the mirror. His jaw was faintly swollen, as if he had mumps on one side, and his chest and rib cage were decorated with purple and blue hoof marks. A few scars added interest to the muscles cording his shoulders and arms, but on the whole he was lean and strong, limber as a whip when he wasn't suffering from bruises and broken bones.

Yes, the man in the mirror looked experienced, if a little worse for wear. Confident, tough as whit leather...as long as you didn't look too closely. Those blue eyes held secrets that made one wonder. Brody blinked hard, deliberately blurring his reflection. He'd been running from that shiftless phony in the mirror for fourteen years, but he always seemed to catch up to him. Every now and then Brody was able to forget the past for days, sometimes weeks at a time, and he thought maybe it was finally coming together for him. But it never really did. There were mistakes that could never be put right. The monster of guilt had sunk its sharp teeth into Brody Walker a long time ago and wasn't about to let go.

Brody turned away from the mirror, rubbing the knot of muscles at the back of his neck with his hand. He went to the bedroom and stretched out on the double bed to wait for Isabelle. His ribs seemed to be crowding his lungs, and he couldn't get comfortable. He turned on his right side and gasped with pain. He rolled over on his left side and his nose bumped into something. Something warm. Something breathing. Something that smelled like violets.

"Why, Izzy B," Brody breathed softly, running his hand over her shoulder. She had changed into something soft and lacy, and Brody ran his fingers over the delicate pattern like a blind man reading Braille. Lace. It wasn't Isabelle's usual style. She favored jeans and brightly colored cotton blouses tied above the midriff. Brody held himself still while he rubbed the lightweight material between his thumb and index finger, listening to the even rise and fall of her breathing. She was asleep.

"We can't have that," Brody murmured, raising up on one elbow, his hand smoothing over her stomach. He found a row of tiny buttons and gently began unfastening them. Isabelle was lying on her back, dead to the world. Any second now she would stir beneath his touch, open her sleepy blue eyes and gasp in sweet surprise. Sweet, sweet surprise...

He worked the buttons one at a time, all the way up to the last one at her throat. Funny. It wasn't like Izzy to wear something buttoned all the way to her neck. She never had much use for buttons.

He slipped his hand beneath the material of her shirt, lightly massaging the silky skin above her waistband. She sighed in her sleep, lifting her arms above her head, a wispy white bra gleaming in the shadows. Brody grinned, thinking Isabelle might not be sleeping as soundly as he'd thought. His hand moved slowly over her rib cage, his fingers brushing the warm underside of her breast. "Sweetheart... Isabelle..."

"Mmm..." She stretched and arched her back, thrusting her breasts forward. Brody grinned. Isabelle was definitely waking up.

"I do love the way you dance," Brody whispered, his hand cupping and lifting the fullness of her breast. So warm, so heavy, so soft...beckoning him. He bent his head, his mouth closing over her nipple through the thin fabric, suckling ever so gently. Her skin had the scent and taste of violets, sweet and distinctive. She sighed again and he lifted his head slightly. His breath came in painful inhalations, which was to be expected with cracked ribs, but his body was hardening with an urgency that surprised him. He lowered his head, pressing warm open kisses on her neck through the silky curtain of her hair. Such beautiful hair, so cool and sleek and smooth...

He froze. Something was wrong here. This was not Isabelle's brand-new curly mane of hair.

This was not Isabelle.

Caitlyn Wilde was having a dream.

Not a bad dream, either; certainly better than anything else that had happened to her in the past three miserable days. She was sleeping in her lovely pedestal bed in the penthouse high atop the Las Brisas Hotel, swathed in cool silk and peach satin. She was waiting for Prince Charming to kiss her awake, and he did...but not on the lips.

It was a lovely dream, but that kiss had been very real and shockingly intimate, and her body had responded with intense pleasure. Not the hazy, fleeting pleasure of a fantasy, but a muscle-tightening, skin-tingling reaction that set off warning bells in her head. She forced her eyelids open and stared at the shadow frozen above her, felt the burning imprint of a man's body from her chest to her toes. Prince Charming was sharing her bed in the penthouse high above the Las Brisas Hotel. Prince Charming smelled of cologne. Prince Charming had his hand on her breast.

This was no dream.

The scream came first, before she could force her weighted limbs to struggle. It was a surprisingly good scream for a woman who was still half-asleep and scared out of her wits—bloodcurdling, in fact. Halfway through it a hand slapped over her mouth, reducing the scream to a muffled whimper.

"I'm not going to jail in Ticaboo, Arizona," a man's voice growled in her ear, "so stop your screaming before the manager comes running in here with a gun. I don't know who the hell you are, Goldilocks, but you're sleeping in *my* bed. Now, do you want to calm down and explain yourself, or do you want to get all hysterical and make things worse?"

Ticaboo, Caitlyn thought, her sleepy mind catching up with her body. Dear heaven, she wasn't in her bed at Las Brisas. She was in some sleazy motel room in a tiny little town called Ticaboo. There was no one to come to her rescue here. She had only herself to depend on to survive her latest blunder. And what a blunder it was.

He seemed to be waiting for her to calm down. Caitlyn forced herself to lie still, her heart slamming painfully against her chest. When he took his hand away from her mouth, she exploded into a hysterical frenzy, shrieking at the top of her lungs, legs and arms flailing, nails digging. Every indignity and disappointment she had suffered in the past three days came to the surface, fueling her rage and panic. Her opponent lost his advantage for a moment; he only had two hands, and one of them was clamped over her mouth again in two seconds. Finally he lunged on top of her, catching her arms above her head with his free hand and pinning her legs with his.

"Get a grip, lady," he gasped, sticking his nose in her face for emphasis. "You try a stunt like that again and I'll truss you up like a side of beef and hang you in the closet. Got it?"

His eyes were mere slits of glittering fury in the shadows. Caitlyn nodded, struggling for breath beneath his hand. It came to her that this man threatening to hang her in the closet was naked. There was a towel scrunched up between them at neck level, a towel that must have covered him at one point.

She squeezed her eyes closed tightly against the frustrated tears that threatened. Her chest heaved, a pathetic little gurgle bubbling up in her throat. Her nose filled up, cutting off the last of her oxygen. She would die here in Ticaboo, Arizona. What a terrible, tiny little place to die. And all because she had wanted to lie down and rest for just a second. It was so unfair.

"Don't cry." There was an unmistakable warning in his voice, the tone of a man who didn't wish to deal with anything more than he was dealing with already. "Lady, if you start crying, I swear I'll... look, listen to me. *Listen.* I'm not going to hurt you.

Hell, I'm the one that should be crying. You broke into my motel room, planted yourself in my bed, made me think you were Isabelle and then scared the bejesus out of—*ouch!*''

Desperate for air, Caitlyn had sunk her teeth into his finger, drawing blood. He whipped his hand away and she sucked oxygen into her burning lungs, sobbing and choking. ''Get off me,'' she gasped when she could finally talk. ''You miserable naked lecher, *get off me!*''

He hesitated for a moment, then surprised her by grabbing the towel and standing up. Although it was too dark to see much of anything, Caitlyn averted her eyes as he knotted the towel around his waist. Her breath came in hard, painful shocks. Here was another fine mess she'd gotten herself into. He was going to want explanations.

''You have some explaining to do,'' he said flatly.

Caitlyn scrambled to sit up, and her blouse fell open. She gave a choked exclamation and started buttoning. ''What do you mean, I have some explaining to do?'' she asked, hoping to put him on the defensive. ''I'm not the one who ripped your clothes off. I should have you arrested. Will you turn around?''

''Lady, even if I could see anything, it wouldn't be anything I haven't seen before. And I wasn't ripping—*removing*—your clothes, I was removing Isabelle's clothes. Or at least I thought I was. And why the hell am I explaining anything?'' he added, raising his voice irritably. "You're the one who broke into my motel room."

"I didn't break in," Caitlyn muttered, buttoning her collar in a choke-hold around her neck. "You can't break into a room that isn't locked in the first place."

"All right, you walked in. I could still have you arrested for trespassing."

"And I could have you arrested for assault!"

"I wasn't assaulting you, I was assaulting Isabelle!" He swore and snatched the Gideon Bible off the nightstand, flinging it across the room. The Bible thumped against the wall near the light switch, and the light globe swinging from the ceiling suddenly came to life.

For a moment, Caitlyn was blinded by the light. She blinked furiously, her heart climbing from her stomach straight into her throat as the man in the towel took shape before her. His damp hair was curling wildly around his face, cut short at the sides, longer and curlier in the back. Wet, it was the color of strong coffee, dry it was probably more gold than brown. His heavy-lidded eyes were blue, not a gentle gray-blue, but a stabbing, electric blue that blazed in his narrow, sun-browned face. Although he had a slender build, his shoulders were broad and sloping and his chest well defined with rippling, tough muscles. His right side was a startling rainbow of odd-shaped bruises, from his collarbone to his waist. He looked like a man who had a great deal of exercise and a very short temper. Caitlyn decided she had made a poor choice of rooms to borrow.

"I think I'll leave now," she said nervously. "We wouldn't want Isabelle to walk in on us, would we?"

He grabbed her upper arm as she swung her legs off the bed. "Sit tight, sweetheart. You aren't going anywhere till we get a few things cleared up."

"You can't keep me here," Caitlyn retorted, a shaky belligerence in her voice. There was only so much misery a woman could take in three days, and she had already more than filled her quota. "I could have you arrested for kidnapping. I could have you arrested for—"

"Oh, hell, don't start that again." He shoved his free hand through his hair, scowling at her. "Look, we didn't get off to a real promising beginning here, but I swear it's going to get worse if you don't cooperate. Who are you?"

Caitlyn realized this was one situation she would have to get out of using ingenuity and resourcefulness. A fresh wave of panic swept through her at the thought. She'd never thought of herself as being particularly ingenious or resourceful. "My name is..." *Think, think, come up with a name*... "Jane Doherty. I saw you leave earlier, and I noticed there was no lock on your door, and I needed someplace to... to..."

"Burglarize?"

"Hide." Her nervous fingers plucked pyramids out of the chenille bedspread. It was difficult to be ingenious and resourceful when his little white towel and all the things it covered were only inches from her nose. "I was out with my boyfriend and he got a little . . . you know, a little . . ."

"The suspense is killing me."

"Too friendly. So I got out of the car and ran away from him and hid behind the soda machine out front. Then I saw you leave your room, so I decided to wait in here until he got tired of looking for me and went home. Ordinarily I wouldn't have done a thing like that, just walking into someone's hotel room, but I was terribly upset."

"Then to calm your nerves you stretched out on the bed and took a little nap. What a crock." He gave a long, put-upon sigh, then spoke in a carefully measured tone. "All right, Jane Doe-er-tee. I don't know whether you're a sleepy thief or a well-dressed runaway or a real shy hooker, but it's a moot point now. I'm going into the bathroom to put on some clothes, and I'd be tickled pink if you weren't here when I came back. Isabelle should be here any minute. She doesn't bite, and I really like that in a woman. Adios."

Caitlyn couldn't believe it. He was letting her go. She watched with saucer eyes as he turned and walked into the bathroom, hips rolling, towel flapping to near-indecency, as nonchalantly as you please. She swallowed hard as he closed the door behind him, feeling as if she had just awakened from a bad dream and couldn't quite get her bearings. What now? Where did she go from here?

She glanced at the window. The gingham curtains were parted a few inches, and rain was striking the window in gusty blasts. The wind sounded almost...demonic, rattling the door in its frame and whistling through the cracks in the walls. She thought about tornadoes, which was ridiculous, because they didn't have tornadoes in Arizona. Did they?

And this was getting her nowhere. She scrambled off the bed, tucking her blouse into her slacks with stiff and clumsy fingers. Her mind replayed the intimate caress given her by a perfect stranger, and her blood burned. A man whose name she didn't even know, who might be an ax murderer or an escaped convict or heaven knew what else, had touched her *there,* and put his lips *there....*

Caitlyn was having a very bad day. The worst in her life, in fact, and there was no end in sight. She slashed at the tears that blurred her vision as she walked over to the door, preparing herself to face the deluge outside. She squared her shoulders and took a deep breath that sounded suspiciously like a sob. Once she walked out of this room she would be at the mercy of the elements. Alone and friendless, without a penny to her name. She was going to get very wet and very cold. She would probably catch pneumonia and die, which wasn't all bad, because at least then she would be out of her misery. There, now she had something to look forward to.

Her fingers closed over the knob on the door and turned it. The instant the latch clicked, a wild gust of wind caught the door and flung it inward. Caitlyn was standing with her right foot slightly in front of her left; otherwise, the door would have caught her full in the face and knocked her cold. As it was, the bottom of the door slammed into her toes with the force of a jackhammer.

The pain was incredible. All five toes on her right foot throbbed in burning, agonizing unison. Caitlyn let out a strangled shriek as she bounced on one foot, her hands going to her hair and tugging, tugging, tugging. She couldn't take any more. She wanted revenge against the fates. She wanted to throw something. She wanted to *explode*.

And so she did.

The door was swinging wildly on its hinges, rain puddling on the speckled tile floor. She picked up the Bible near her feet and sent it flying into the stormy night. She kicked a round tin wastebasket with her good foot, then hopped around the floor after it so she could kick it again and again, until she kicked it right out the door. She grabbed an ashtray off the dresser and tossed it outside with an angry sob, then spotted the pile of wet clothes near the door. *His* clothes, that blue-eyed naked person who had threatened her and mocked her and dismissed her so callously. She was going for the cowboy boots when she heard the pained voice behind her.

"Man, this sort of thing never happens at Howard Johnson's."

Caitlyn swung around with a small, choked gasp. Blue Eyes had exchanged his towel for jeans and was shrugging into a blue and white plaid shirt. He winced as he eased his right arm into the sleeve. "Lady, you're completely ruining my night, you know that?"

She stared at him, her chest heaving.

"I should have known." He took a deep breath, then expelled it. "It's always the sweet, delicate-looking types that give you hell."

Caitlyn blinked in slow motion, touching the heat stains on her cheeks. Now she'd done it. Now he would call the police, or maybe he would just strangle her on the spot and bury her out behind the soda machine. "Dear heaven," she whispered hoarsely. "What have I done?"

He walked to the open doorway, squinting into the darkness. "You killed the trash can," he said. He turned his head, studied her pale face for a moment, then sighed again and kicked the door shut with his bare foot. "It's raining pretty hard out there. Maybe you should—hell, I can't believe I'm saying this—maybe you should hang around for a little while until it lets up."

Caitlyn slumped against the wall, palms spread flat on either side of her hips. Across the room she caught her reflection in the cracked mirror above the dresser. Tangled auburn hair, dark, wet eyes that ate up her whole face, lips that quivered like a worn out baby's. She looked lost. She felt lost.

"I have places to go," she said dully, because she didn't want this blue-eyed cowboy to know how desperate she really was. "I have things to do. Besides, you don't want me here. Isabelle's coming."

He nodded. "You're right. I don't want you here. I didn't want to get my ribs cracked last Friday night, either, but it happened anyway. Some things you just have to deal with."

She lifted her chin, trying to control her trembling lower lip. "Well, you don't have to deal with me. I can take care of myself. I'm leaving now."

Obligingly he stepped aside, opening a path to the door. Caitlyn hesitated, but only for a moment. She brushed her hair out of her eyes, turned to look for her purse—then remembered she didn't have one anymore. Trying to hold herself with as much dignity as possible, she walked past him to the door. She would leave and she would leave with her head held high. Once outside, she would lay down in the muddy parking lot and cry. It was good to have a plan.

"Don't be a stranger," he called after her.

For the first time in her life, Caitlyn had the urge to make an obscene finger gesture, but she didn't want to further humiliate herself by using the wrong finger. Her hand closed around the door knob.

"Bye now," he said.

Caitlyn glanced over her shoulder. He was standing with his thumbs hooked in his pockets, his shirt hanging open over his jeans. His hair had dried to a warm honey color, curling like a halo around his golden face. He was rocking up and down on the balls of his feet, and he seemed to be enjoying himself. "I pity Isabelle," she said by way of a parting shot.

His smile stretched wickedly, blue eyes gleaming. "Don't."

Caitlyn threw open the door, stepped outside and slammed it behind her. Before she could take another step she was completely drenched, her hair sticking to her face, a wild wind trying to strip the clothes from her body. She couldn't see beyond a slanting wall of rain, couldn't hear anything above the thunder rolling over the pines. She told herself it was all right to cry now, because she no longer had an audience. Tears and raindrops mingled as she stood there on the wooden step in front of the Ticaboo Tourist Lodge. She cried for all her lost dreams and bitter disappointments. She cried for her broken toes. She cried for her soaking wet white leather sandals that would never be the same.

Suddenly the door flew open behind her. A hand closed around the back of her neck and pulled her into the room. "It's always the delicate-looking ones," her reluctant savior muttered, slamming the door closed with a force that put the thunder to shame. "What were you going to do, stand out there and howl in the rain all night long?"

"I don't know." Caitlyn shook her head, staring at him through a haze of tears and misery. All the anger had gone out of her, replaced by exhaustion and discouragement. "I really don't know what I was going to do."

He put his hand in the middle of her back and pushed her toward the bed. "Sit. Don't look at me like that, I'm not going to attack you. Look in the mirror if you don't believe me."

She looked in the mirror. Her hair was sticking to her head and neck like wet seaweed. Her mascara was running in black rivers down her cheeks and dripping off her chin. Her lace blouse had stretched out to size extra large and was hanging off one shoulder.

She gave a strangled cry and sat on the edge of the bed. A minute later a towel was pushed into her hands.

"Here. See what you can do with that."

Caitlyn buried her sullied face in the rough terry cloth. "This is so humiliating," she mumbled hoarsely. "All I wanted to do was rest for a minute. I was so tired...I must have walked ten miles. I never meant to fall asleep. I never meant to have my purse stolen, either. I don't know why these things keep happening to me. I don't know where I'm going, I don't know how I'm going to get there...I don't know anything."

"Don't you think you're being a little hard on yourself?"

Her breath caught on a sob. "It's the truth."

"You know how to trash a motel room," he pointed out.

Caitlyn came out of the towel, glaring at him with swollen eyes. "Thank you. I feel so much better."

He sat beside her on the bed, keeping a good six inches between himself and the damp patch spreading beneath his guest. "I know it's none of my business, but it's pretty obvious you've gotten yourself into some kind of a mess here. I can understand if you don't want to talk about it, but maybe there's something I can do to help you out."

"Why would you want to help me?" she asked in a soggy voice.

He shrugged. "I've hit rock bottom a few times myself. I know what it's like."

"You don't even know me."

"I know your name isn't Jane Doherty."

Caitlyn hesitated, looking at him warily. "No, it isn't. How did you know?"

"Never try to kid a kidder," he said, holding out his hand. "Brody Walker. And you're?"

"Caitlyn Wilde," she said, briefly putting her cold hand in his. Actually she was cold all over. Icicle chills flickered up and down her spine. She would have given everything she owned—which at the moment was absolutely nothing—for a cup of hot coffee.

"See how easy that was? We've exchanged formal introductions and shared a bed, though not in that order. We're practically bosom buddies."

Caitlyn pulled her hand away, acutely uncomfortable with the topic of bosoms. "Not quite. And we didn't *share* a bed, we bumped into each other *in* a bed. There's a big difference."

"Details. Women always get hung up on details." Brody shook his head, leaning back on his elbows. He was quiet for a moment. "Caitlyn?"

"What?"

"You haven't eaten for a while, have you?"

Caitlyn bit down on her lower lip. She'd hoped the sound of her stomach growling would be lost in the thunder. "Not since breakfast . . . yesterday."

"Yesterday?" Brody repeated, tipping back his head and looking down his nose at her. "You haven't had anything to eat since yesterday? Hell, no wonder you killed the trash can. Starvation makes people irritable." He got off the bed, picking up the wet cowboy boots from the floor. "I'll tell you what. Bird's Café is closed now, but there's a convenience store across the street. I'll go pick you up a nice assortment of junk food. You'll have a terrific sugar rush and you'll start feeling like a new woman."

"You don't need to do that," Caitlyn said, salivating at the thought of a candy bar.

"Code of the West, ma'am," Brody said, taking the chair near the door while he tugged on his boots. "If you find a starving woman hiding out in your motel room, you have to feed her, no questions asked. Aargh, that hurts. *Damn* that horse.''

''What horse?'' Caitlyn asked, tired and confused.

''The one that stomped on me at the rodeo last Friday. Getting in and out of these boots is killing me. I'm going to have to swallow my pride and buy some sneakers.'' He stood up, pulling a silver windbreaker off the back of the chair and putting it on. ''I'll be right back. If you want to get out of those wet clothes, there's a robe hanging on the back of the bathroom door.''

''The clothes stay on,'' Caitlyn muttered, trying not to catch her tongue in her chattering teeth.

''Suit yourself.'' He sent her a lazy grin over his shoulder, pulling the door open. ''You'd be happier with your clothes off, though.''

''Aren't we all?'' a third voice drawled.

Brody's head swiveled as he stared at the woman standing in the open doorway, her hand raised to knock. She wore a yellow rain slicker with the hood pulled over her eyes to protect her new permanent.

''Isabelle,'' Brody said.

A red-rimmed smile flashed within the shadows of the rain slicker. ''Hello, darlin'. I believe I caught you at a bad time.''

On the bed, Caitlyn turned every shade of red, trying furiously to rearrange her dripping, slipping blouse. Brody threw her a quelling look, then smiled at Isabelle. '' 'Caught' isn't the word I'd use, Izzy.

Come on in out of the rain, and we'll talk. We have ourselves a little situation here.''

"Oh, I can't stay," Isabelle replied sweetly, wiggling her fingers at Caitlyn over Brody's shoulder. "Hello, there. Aren't you a pretty thing?" Then, to Brody, "This won't take but a second of your precious time. I just wanted to give you a little something."

Before Brody could blink, Isabelle's fist shot out of the rain slicker, catching him hard in the ribs. He gasped and doubled over, staggering backward. Isabelle smiled at Caitlyn.

"He's all yours, honey," she said.

Two

Hurricane Isabelle left a puddle of rainwater on the floor, and the sound of a door slamming reverberated through the room.

"Brody?" Caitlyn whispered apprehensively, staring at his frozen, crippled posture.

"What?" His voice was thready but calm.

"Are you all right?"

He nodded, still clutching his middle. "You bet. Doing fine."

Caitlyn swallowed hard and climbed off the bed. "Is there anything I can do?" She approached him cautiously, not at all sure he would appreciate comfort from her at this particular moment. "Brody, I'm

so sorry. Do you want me to go after her and bring
her back?''

''Lord, no.''

She bit her lip, patting him awkwardly on the
shoulder. ''I know this is my fault. If she hadn't seen
me, she wouldn't have jumped to conclusions and
she wouldn't have turned on you like that. I've never
seen a woman get so...physical. She might not bite,
but she has a heck of a right hook. Where are you
going?'' This she asked as Brody turned toward the
bed in slow motion. ''Can I help you?''

He shook his head, planting one foot in front of
the other with grim determination. ''You've done so
much already. I'll just stretch out on the bed for a
few minutes till I have the will to live again.''

''I guess I'll leave, then,'' she said miserably.

''Don't do that.'' Brody bit his lip as he lowered
himself onto the bed, his face nearly the same color
as the gray chenille spread. ''If you run off into the
storm, I have to go running after you. Code of the
West, article two.''

Caitlyn smiled faintly, though she felt more like
crying. ''You couldn't run if you tried. You're inca-
pacitated.''

''But I probably *would* try, because I can't resist a
damsel in distress, and it would hurt like hell.'' He
lay on his back, eyes closed, arms straight at his
sides, cowboy boots hanging off the end of the bed.
''Do me a favor and stay put, all right? Just give me
a few minutes to compose myself here.''

"I feel terrible," Caitlyn muttered, wringing her hands.

"Don't we all," he said with feeling.

Caitlyn took the chair near the door and moved it to a dry spot near the radiator. She studied his motionless figure with anxious eyes for what seemed a long time, resisting the urge to jump up and check his breathing. Well, she thought bleakly, what would she do if he did stop breathing? Could she give him mouth to mouth or CPR or whatever it was a person did in these circumstances? No, because Caitlyn Wilde didn't know the difference between CPR and TNT. She was totally useless, unless the ability to draw disaster like a magnet counted for something.

She slumped in her chair, feeling a sickening, apprehensive knot twisting and tightening in her stomach. It was all going so terribly wrong. All she had wanted was a little freedom, a chance to finally prove herself. Well, she had certainly done that. She had proven once and for all that she was completely and totally inept. She had always known she was a dreamer, but she had liked to believe she had the ability to make some of those dreams come true. All she had wanted was a chance.

She looked at the telephone on the nightstand, her lips compressing tightly. She could call Nicky now, and it would all be over. The frustration. The humiliation. The disappointment. The danger to innocent bystanders like Brody Walker.

And the dreams, she thought wistfully. The adventure, the possibilities....

"You still there?" Brody mumbled, his lips barely moving.

Caitlyn jumped up from her chair and crossed to the bed. "Yes, I'm right here. Do you need something? Can I get you anything?"

"Tell me something."

"What?"

"How did a nice girl like you end up in a place like this?"

She shrugged, clasping and unclasping her hands. "It's a long story with a sad ending. You don't want to hear it."

"Not if you don't want to tell it." His eyes remained closed. "Would you mind putting another pillow under my head?"

"Of course." Grateful for something useful to do, she pulled the extra pillow from beneath the bedspread and placed it gently under his head. "There. Is that better?"

"Much. Except for..."

"Except for what?" Caitlyn touched his honey-colored hair uncertainly, wanting to offer some sort of comfort. The curls were baby-fine beneath her fingertips, cool and silky to the touch. "Are you in pain?"

"Well..." He was quiet for a moment, then sighed and looked up at her with haunting, crystalline-blue eyes. His wide mouth lifted at the corners in a faint, courageous smile. "It's not too bad. I think if I could get these boots off, I'd be a little more comfortable. Would you mind?"

"Mind?" Caitlyn turned her head, her eyes skimming down his long legs to the scuffed leather cowboy boots. "No, of course I don't mind if you take them off." Heaven knew she'd seen him in less.

"I'm not sure I can," he said slowly. "At least, not by myself. If you could just stand down there at the bottom of the bed . . ."

"Oh. Well, sure." Caitlyn moved to the end of the bed, staring at the boots with a bemused expression. She rubbed her hands together, then gripped both heels.

"No, not like that," Brody said. "You have to turn around."

"Turn around? How can I pull off your boots if I'm facing the opposite direction?"

He lifted himself up on his elbows with a grimace of pain. "You stand—wait, I need to catch my breath here—you stand with my foot between your legs. Then you take the boot firmly by the heel and pull it up and off. It'll work like a charm, I promise."

"I see." Caitlyn turned slowly, then looked over her shoulder at Brody. "You're quite sure this is the way it's done?"

"I've been getting in and out of these things for years. This is exactly the way you go about it, believe me."

His Western drawl seemed to have suddenly become more pronounced, and Caitlyn stared at him suspiciously. He returned her look with bright-eyed innocence, his rueful, self-conscious smile thrown slightly off center by his swollen jaw. "I wouldn't ask if I could do it myself," he said.

Caitlyn took a deep breath, then stepped gingerly over his left foot, positioning the cowboy boot between her legs. She bent over, getting a firm grip on the heel with both hands. "Like this?"

"Yes, ma'am—exactly like that."

"All right. I'll try to be gentle so I don't hurt you." And she did, but the darn boot wouldn't budge. She tried again, with as much strength as she dared, but met with the same results.

"Guess my foot must be swollen up," Brody murmured sadly. "I took a pretty bad fall at that rodeo. Why don't you give it a real firm tug this time?"

"I don't want to hurt you."

"I can handle it."

She wrestled with his boot for another couple of minutes before the light dawned. Each time she pulled, Brody tightened up his foot, preventing the boot from coming off. Caitlyn closed her eyes and counted to ten. She should have known. Those blue eyes were just too bright, the smile too innocent, the cherub curls too, too adorable. She hoped he was enjoying the view of her posterior, because it was going to cost him dearly. "Maybe I'll just tug a little harder," she said sweetly, her voice dripping with her very own brand-new Western drawl. She glanced over her shoulder and smiled at Brody. His dreamy expression changed to one of wide-eyed apprehension.

"Caitlyn, I think I can—"

"One, two...*three.*" She jerked the boot upward with all her might, mind and heart. Behind her she heard Brody yelp with pain as he fell against the mattress. The boot came off like a charm, just as he'd promised. She only wished it could have been his head. "Nothing to it," she announced cheerfully, tossing the boot into the corner and rubbing her hands together. "Let's get the other one off, shall we? I think I've got the hang of it now."

"I'll do it myself," Brody snapped, his head buried in pillows. "What the hell are you trying to do, finish the job Isabelle started?"

"I'd love to," Caitlyn said, turning on him with dark eyes flashing. "But I've wasted enough time with you and your idiotic code of the West. You're an opportunist, Brody Walker."

"Which makes me a fairly normal male," he pointed out irritably.

"Well, I wouldn't brag about it. You know, I actually thought you were sincere about offering your help, no strings attached. You'd think I'd finally wise up after everything that's happened the last couple of days. First that horrid truck driver steals my purse. Then that aluminum siding salesman dumps me in the middle of nowhere because I wouldn't . . . well, it just goes to show you how gullible I am. Nicky was right. I'm not capable of making my own decisions. I'm an *idiot*."

Brody lifted his head off the pillow. "Who the hell is Nicky?"

"Never mind who Nicky is. I'm leaving."

"Hold it." He swung his legs off the bed, gasping as the sudden movement robbed him of breath. "Caitlyn...I was only teasing you. Don't get all riled up. I'm not going to jump your bones at the Ticaboo Tourist Lodge."

"You're right," Caitlyn shot back, "because I'm leaving the Ticaboo Tourist Lodge before you get the chance." She marched to the door with Brody and his remaining cowboy boot hobbling after her. "Happy trails, pilgrim. Next time I hope the horse sits on you."

"Look, I was just admiring the scenery. Since when was that a crime? There's no reason for you to—"

Brody Walker got the door slammed in his face for the third time that night. Caitlyn had nothing more to say to him, or any other man who walked the face of the earth. Except one. It was time to admit defeat. In three short days she had lost everything she had to lose, which was probably some sort of world record. The cheerful optimism that had prompted her adventure had died a painful death.

She hardly felt the rain stinging her face as she trudged through the muddy parking lot toward the lighted phone booth in front of the manager's office. She closed herself inside the bright little box, her fingers shaking as she dialed the operator and asked to make a collect call.

"Whom should I say is calling?" the operator asked after she took the number.

Caitlyn leaned against the glass wall, closing her eyes tiredly. "Just tell him it's an orphan of the storm."

Nicky answered halfway through the first ring, accepting the charges in a tight voice she recognized only too well. He must have been sitting on the telephone, and here it was nearly two in the morning.

"Hello?" he repeated. "Cat? Is that you?"

She opened her mouth to pour out her woes, to shift all her grief and misery to her stepbrother's capable shoulders. It was something she had done most of her life, allowing Nicky to fight her battles and slay her dragons and keep her shielded from harsh reality. It was second nature now.

"*Cat*. Are you all right?"

"I'm all right," she said tiredly.

"Where the hell are you?"

All she had to do was tell him. She would be rescued from the big nasty world of dishonest truck drivers and slimy aluminum siding salesmen and opportunistic, blue-eyed cowboys. All she had to do was tell him where she was. He would take care of her and coddle her and make very sure nothing like this ever happened to her again.

"I'm all right," she said again.

"I've had my people searching for you for the past three days. I've been half out of my mind with worry. You can't just disappear like this. There are people here who care about you. You owe them something."

By "them" he meant himself, Caitlyn thought. It was a priority with Nicky Shapiro, the sacred obligation to family.

Suddenly she was too weary to stand. Her back propped against the wall, she sank slowly to the dirty floor of the phone booth until her knees were tucked beneath her chin. "I didn't mean to worry you. I didn't plan on leaving like that, I just . . . had an impulse. I needed to try my wings, Nicky. Just once."

"And you're ready to come home now." It wasn't a question. It was a statement of fact, delivered with quiet authority.

"Nicky . . ."

"Tell me where you are, Cat. I'll come and get you."

"I can't do that," Caitlyn whispered, realizing with a little shock that she still had some fight left in her. She, who had never in her life been forced to depend on her fragile little self, was somehow going to find her way out of this muddy, dead-end town. She was going to get on her feet again—if she could pry herself off the bubble gum on the floor of the phone booth—and she was going to forge ahead. She was going to discover what was around the next bend, and the bend after that. She might be inexperienced, insecure and naive, but she was determined.

"What do you mean, you can't do that?" Nicky roared.

"I'm not giving up yet," Caitlyn said, feeling an odd, inexplicable surge of pride wash deep down within her. Lord knew she didn't have anything to be proud of at this stage of the game. "I'll call you when I get settled, Nicky."

"Settled? What the hell do you mean, settled? Like finding a job, an apartment? You're twenty-two years old, Caitlyn. Don't you think that's a little old to be running away from home? When are you going to grow up?"

"I think I started tonight," Caitlyn said, watching water trickle into the phone booth through what appeared to be a bullet hole. "Believe me, Nicky, there's no place for me to go from here but up."

There was a long pause. "I didn't realize your life here was so terrible."

Guilt. Nicky was a master when it came to manipulating people. It was one of the reasons he was one of the wealthiest, most powerful hoteliers in Las Vegas. It was also one of the reasons Caitlyn had fled from his smothering influence. It had become impossible to distinguish which thoughts were her own and which were Nicky's. "I have to go," she said quickly, before he could change her mind. She struggled to her feet, pulling a face as she brushed unidentified sticky things off the seat of her pants. "I'll call. Don't worry about me."

"Caitlyn, don't you dare hang up on me."

She hung up on him, because she didn't know what else to do. Almost immediately she felt herself getting light-headed, and she had to concentrate on breathing deeply and evenly. What had she done? Well, she'd committed herself to spending the night in a telephone booth, for one thing. Allowed her heart to rule her head, for another. And most distressing of all, she had alienated the only family she had in the world.

She'd told Nicky she would call him when she got settled, but she had no idea how to go about getting settled. She would have to find a job, but she didn't have any work experience. And an apartment, though she had no idea where she would get the money for the first month's rent.

She drooped her forehead against the telephone and closed her eyes. "If ignorance is bliss," she muttered, "I must be the happiest person on earth."

Since she had no pressing engagements, she stayed where she was, watching the rain trickle down and waiting for a flash of inspiration to indicate her next move. She was thinking how nice it would be if she could sleep standing up, like a horse did, when Brody Walker suddenly pushed the door open, ducking his head into the lighted booth. Dripping curls were plastered to his forehead like little question marks.

His windbreaker was shiny wet and billowed open in the gusty wind.

He raised his voice to be heard over the noise of the storm. "If you knew what a pain it was for me to pull on that damn boot again, you'd be ashamed of yourself. What are you doing in here?"

Caitlyn shrugged. She needed a little time to plan her next move. "What are you doing out there?"

"What do you think I'm doing out here? I'm rescuing distressed damsels from telephone booths." He jumped as the sky suddenly split open with sound and fury, white lightning flashing a noonday brilliance on the muddy scene. Three seconds later Brody was inside the booth with Caitlyn, pushing the door closed with the heel of his boot. It was the only way to accomplish the task in such crowded quarters.

"Dangerous business, rescuing distressed damsels," he muttered breathlessly, wiping the water from his eyes. "It's not easy, being a hero."

Caitlyn pressed herself backward, futilely trying to put some distance between herself and this dripping cowboy. "No one called for a hero."

"No?" He raised his brows innocently, a smile lurking in his blue eyes. "I could have sworn I heard a cry for help in the night. Oh, well. You're about as distressed as I've ever seen a woman, so I may as well rescue you while I'm here."

"I'm not distressed."

"What are you, then?" His bright gaze was inquiring, his head tilted to the side.

A good question, Caitlyn thought, feeling the telephone receiver digging into the small of her back. What was she? "I'm just...alone," she said finally. "That's the way I want it. Why don't you go check the telephone booth down the street? Maybe you can find someone else to rescue."

He looked at her with a mildly aggravated expression. "Well, that's gratitude for you. I tell you, the hero business isn't what it's cracked up to be."

"Neither are the heroes," Caitlyn mumbled, intensely conscious of the tips of her breasts grazing his chest. No matter which way she wiggled, the only available room for her slight body seemed to be within the cradle of his hips.

"You probably shouldn't squirm around like that," he said, frowning thoughtfully. "I've chastised myself for teasing you back in the motel room, and I'm toying with the idea of behaving myself from now on. Your help would be appreciated."

"Your absence would be appreciated," Caitlyn said in a tight, shaky voice. Despite the storm, the temperature in the telephone booth suddenly seemed to be rising. There also seemed to be a lack of oxygen, despite the ventilation from the bullet hole. "You're giving me claustrophobia."

He shook his head, giving her a faint, inscrutable smile. He opened his mouth and said something, but the words were lost in the sepulcharal shock of angry thunder. Rain struck the glass in blasts and a keening wind rattled the door.

Neither moved, partly because there was nowhere to go, partly because the crackling tension in the tiny cubicle was suddenly just as unpredictable and startling as the storm blowing around them. Brody's smile faded, and his body was very still, almost rigid.

"Caitlyn," he said quietly, a tiny frown etched between his brows as he stared at her. He looked like a man who was thinking long and hard on a perplexing question. His hand found hers between their bodies, his thumb lightly rubbing the pulse at her wrist.

Caitlyn stared at him for what seemed to be a very long time. His eyes had darkened to a smoky, midnight blue. Water dripped off his lashes, trickling down his face like tears. She wondered if this brash womanizer had ever cried. The mind boggled.

"What are you doing?" she asked, sounding more like a distressed damsel than she would have liked.

"Just coming in out of the rain for a minute," he said quietly. Something in his voice hinted at a bleak irony she couldn't begin to understand. "Just coming in out of the rain."

Caitlyn wet her lips, trying to swallow through a desert-dry throat. He was awfully good at that little-boy-lost routine. Appealing and wistful, with just a hint of vulnerability. She closed her eyes against his calculated charm. She was never going to reach woman-of-the-world status unless she developed a healthy instinct for self-preservation. "I was here first," she said.

His hand released hers. "Don't you know how to share?"

"No."

"I could teach you."

"I'm a slow learner."

"I'm a slow teacher. That's what I call a fortuitous coincidence."

"That's it. I'm leaving." Caitlyn's voice was brittle, on the knife edge of panic. His thighs were yearning against hers, and she burned there. The whole storm-tossed world seemed to be spinning around her, making everything hazy, unreal.

Softly, calmly he asked, "Where are you going to go, Caitlyn?"

She opened her mouth and closed it again. She didn't know. She truly didn't know, and she was too tired to improvise.

"I don't suppose you'd like to share my hotel room?" Brody asked, white teeth flashing. "No, I take that back. For a minute there I forgot that I was behaving myself. Besides, you don't know how to share. Fortunately, I just spoke with the manager here, and he happens to have a vacancy. Seventeen vacancies, actually." He reached into the pocket of his windbreaker, cracking his elbow against the glass in the process. "Ouch! Damn, I hate pain, I really do. Here." Maneuvering rather awkwardly, he brought forth a small paper sack. "I ran over to the store across the street," he said. "They didn't have any honest-to-goodness food, but I got you some candy and some licorice. There's a couple of other things I thought you might need, as well."

Caitlyn's eyes were big as saucers as she peered into the sack. Besides the food, she saw a comb, a toothbrush and toothpaste and a travel-size bottle of moisturizer. She expelled her breath softly as she pulled a giant-sized chocolate bar from the sack. "I think the lightning hit me. I think I've died and gone to heaven."

Brody smiled faintly, pulling a room key from the pocket of his jeans. "The Ticaboo Tourist Lodge is a far cry from heaven," he said, dropping the key into the sack. "You're in number five, right next to mine. First class accommodations, too—you've actually got a lock on your door."

Caitlyn looked from Brody Walker to the chocolate bar and back again. "I have a room here?"

"With any luck, you'll even have clean towels. And if you'll look closely at that key, you'll notice there isn't a single string attached." He tipped up her chin with his finger, pulling her glassy-eyed stare from the candy bar. "Get a good night's rest. I can tell you from personal experience that things always look better in the morning."

A bed. A shower. Three candy bars and a package of licorice. Caitlyn almost cried with joy. "No strings?" she whispered.

He shook his head, wiggling the tip of her nose with his finger. "Not a one. Sometimes I amaze myself, I really do."

Caitlyn stared at him, seeing for the first time in those beautifully chiseled, sun-browned features something she had never noticed before. Gentleness.

She watched as Brody pulled up the collar of his windbreaker and pushed open the door. Water slanted in on them from every direction, and Caitlyn quickly shielded the precious chocolate bar she held in her hand. Brody grinned at her, then ducked into the pouring rain. He turned and waited for her, water vapor swirling around him like smoke.

Waiting to see her safely to her room. Watching over her, just as Nicky had always done. It was that stifling overprotectiveness that had finally driven her away from home, but tonight it was such a relief to know she wasn't completely alone.

I'll be independent tomorrow, she thought. And I'll be darn good at it, too. It's just going to take a little practice.

Head bowed, paper sack clutched against her chest, she dashed into the storm. Lightning split open the sky once again, but she wasn't afraid. Tonight she had found a most unorthodox, irrepressible guardian angel who went by the name of Brody Walker.

Three
___

Brody Walker was no angel.

He knew it, and everyone who knew him knew it. Words like "significant" and "meaningful" made him nervous. He enjoyed friendly relationships with cocktail waitresses and former prom queens from Mexico to Canada, women he could take out to dinner and fuss over and share a good laugh with. Most of the time he was careful to keep his hands to himself and his jeans zipped. He was more interested in distracting himself than indulging himself.

He was fortunate to know one or two women like Isabelle, good friends who didn't expect or want anything more from him than a warm cuddle every now and then. He made himself scarce whenever a

woman got that look in her eye that said she wanted
something from him he didn't have to give. He
wasn't interested in hearts and flowers, and he didn't
believe in happy-ever-after. He liked good times and
new adventures and fresh scenery. He considered a
few dozen broken bones a small price to pay for the
colorful, ever-changing life on the rodeo circuit.

He never worried about his ranch in Wyoming
while he was on the road, since he left little brother
Billy in charge, and Billy was a fairly responsible in-
dividual. He felt sorry for people whose lives passed
by while they were busy setting goals and turning
themselves inside out to meet others' expectations.
He never made long-term plans, and he never made
promises. The way he figured it, the fewer promises
made, the fewer disappointments suffered. Playing
at the hero business was fine and dandy, as long as
no one made the mistake of taking him too seriously. Brody had learned long ago that he wasn't cut
out to save the world. He barely managed to save
himself.

Without a doubt, Brody was no angel...but every
so often he stumbled across a situation that he could
remedy without actually getting himself involved. He
was always willing to lend money to friends, no
questions asked. If he found a stray dog on the road,
he would pay someone in the next town to look after
it. Once he'd come across a twelve-year-old runaway at a rodeo in Sante Fe, a scrawny boy who was
all frightened eyes and bony little ribs. Brody had fed

him and let him bed down in the back of his truck, and by morning he had talked him into accepting a bus ticket home.

Caitlyn Wilde was different. As a charity case, she was dangerous. He'd known it when he'd stood nose to nose with her in that phone booth, and a damn cute little nose she had. She'd looked at him with those dark brown eyes, eyes big enough and deep enough for a man to drown in. And her lower lip... her luscious lower lip had trembled with emotion and exhaustion, no matter how many times she bit down on it. She was mysterious and vulnerable and appealing. She had a feisty streak he thought was adorable, but which probably accounted for a great deal of her troubles, since she was also naive.

In short, she was just the sort of woman he had nightmares about. A woman who made him worry about her.

It wasn't surprising Brody couldn't sleep after he'd seen Caitlyn to her room. He walked around in the rain for a while, until his boots were weighed down with mud and his clammy skin prickled with goose bumps. Too bad the cold didn't seep deep within him, to the fire that had flickered to life around about midnight when he'd cuddled up in bed with his surprise visitor. He couldn't forget the scent of violets in his dark room, or the feel of her silky flesh beneath his seeking hands. The woman had staying power. He was going to have to watch himself.

At last, he went to bed and stubbornly remained there, bright-eyed and bothered, until it was time to get up again. He pulled back the gingham curtains at the window and noticed the storm clouds had cleared. Then he opened the window and stuck his head out, craning his neck to see the window next door. The curtains were closed and all was quiet.

A heavy-set woman carrying a plastic bucket filled with cleaning supplies trudged past him on the wooden porch. Brody got himself quite a look, and he remembered he was stark naked and the window ledge a mere four feet high. He ducked inside and padded toward the bathroom. He'd give Caitlyn another hour of sleep, then buy her a good hot breakfast. After that, he would bid her farewell and ride off into the sunset like a good cowboy should. He didn't mind looking after strays now and again, as long as it was a short-term commitment.

It was exactly eight-thirty when Brody approached her motel room door, dressed in a fresh chambray shirt and jeans. He knocked softly at first, because she'd been as weary as a sparrow blown from its nest last night and was probably sleeping like a baby. Then he knocked a little harder, thinking she might be in the shower. Finally he pounded on the door and shouted her name, but she didn't answer. He was getting worried, which irritated the hell out of him. He walked over to the manager's office and asked for an extra key, then went to Caitlyn's room and let himself in. The covers were thrown off the bed. The towels in the bathroom were damp, the mirror still edged with steam. Obviously she hadn't been gone long, but she *was* gone.

Brody took the key back to the manager, telling himself it was his lucky day. He'd just been spared the expense of Caitlyn's breakfast and probably the price of a bus ticket for her, as well. Wherever she'd gone, whatever she was doing, she was no longer his concern. Not that he ever *was* concerned. Still, he was surprised she hadn't taken the time to thank him. After all, without his help, she'd probably have spent the night in a phone booth.

He decided against breakfast, since he seemed to have lost his appetite. He opened the camper shell on the back of his truck and tossed in his duffel bag with all the force a man with cracked ribs could muster. He figured he would drive straight through to Moab, then take it easy for the rest of the day, maybe bake in the sun beside a motel pool. If he strapped up his ribs real tight, he shouldn't have any problem riding in the Canyonlands Rodeo the next day. And he wouldn't give Caitlyn Wilde another thought, because that was the kind of man he was. Easygoing, with a live-and-let-live attitude.

Still, she might have taken the time to thank him and say goodbye. It would have been the considerate thing to do.

Brody walked around the truck to the driver's side, then noticed a sleek black Jaguar with Nevada license plates parked in front of the manager's office.

The car was a far cry from the dusty pickups and flatbeds he usually saw in little farm towns like Ticaboo. He caught himself wondering if the Jaguar was somehow connected to Caitlyn's sudden flight. Perhaps she was running from something or someone. Perhaps she was in some kind of danger....

Then again, maybe she was paddling with one oar out of the water. He climbed into the truck and slammed the door. He wasn't going to waste his time worrying about a woman he would never see again. Especially a woman who broke into motel rooms, kept him up all night and didn't have the simple decency to say thank you. He didn't need the aggravation.

"Will you start the darn truck already?"

Brody jumped straight off the seat, his knees slamming into the steering wheel. His head swiveled like it was on springs, tawny curls flying. There was a woman snuggled up on the floor of his truck, the same woman who'd been snuggled up in his bed the night before.

"Gosh *damn* it," he hollered, barely able to hear himself over the thudding of his heart. "What the hell do you think you're doing under there? Are you trying to give me a heart attack, or what?"

"Keep your voice down!" Caitlyn squirmed beneath the dashboard, trying to reach the key in the ignition. "I'm here because I need a lift out of town, all right? Will you please start the truck?"

Brody slapped her hand away from the keys. "What's wrong with asking me for a ride instead of hiding in my truck and scaring me to death? What's wrong with sitting on the seat, like a normal person? Do you do *anything* like a normal person?"

She stared at him from her cramped position. "I'm keeping a low profile. Brody, please—let's just get out of here."

"I don't need this," Brody grumbled to himself. But still he started the engine, grinding the gear as he shifted into reverse. As he pulled out of the parking lot, he noticed a dark-haired, slightly overfed bodybuilder type walk out of the manager's office toward the Jaguar. The man wore a perfectly tailored three-piece suit and a disgruntled expression.

"How do you feel about black Jaguars?" Brody asked Caitlyn.

"I'm allergic to them," she said in a suffocated voice.

"So you don't want to stop and say hi? There's a chubby high roller getting into the Jag. Really knows how to dress, too. Maybe you could hitch a ride."

"No." She pressed herself even farther beneath the dashboard. "I like it where I am."

When Brody cruised past the Jaguar, the owner of the car turned and gave him a suspicious once-over. Brody returned the favor, wondering what connection this man had with the woman hiding on the floor of his truck. Family member? Maybe. Private detective? Unlikely, the suit looked too expensive.

Husband? Was this the Nicky Caitlyn had referred to the night before? He didn't look like a Nicky. He looked like a Guido.

Brody glanced at Caitlyn, noticing for the first time the expensive diamond studs in her ears. The lace blouse and white pants she wore were atrociously wrinkled, victims of a motel sink washing, but he would have bet his last pain pill they bore designer labels. Her freshly shampooed hair crackled in a flyaway curtain around her face, a heavy fringe of bangs tangling with her eyelashes, but the cut appeared highly professional. He figured she would look right at home in the front seat of a Jaguar once she was spruced up a little.

He pulled out onto the main road, grinding the gears once again as he shifted into third. He didn't need the aggravation.

"Where are we?" Caitlyn asked.

"Driving down the road," Brody snapped. He was still visualizing Mr. and Mrs. Guido snuggled up together in the Jaguar.

"Is he following us?"

"Is who following us?"

"You know. Him. The man in the black Jaguar."

"Oh, him." Brody looked in his rearview mirror and saw a dusty cattle truck lumbering behind them. "Yeah, he's right on our tail. You better stay put."

Caitlyn subsided into silence. Brody took a deep, hard breath and stomped on the accelerator, wondering why on earth he was so damned relieved to see her again.

They drove for ten or fifteen minutes before Caitlyn started to giggle. Lord knew there was nothing to giggle about, but she couldn't help it. She was sitting on the floor of a pickup truck, hiding from Lyle Switzer, Nicky's lumbering, muscle-bound executive assistant. Her underwear was still uncomfortably damp from being washed the night before. She had had nothing to eat in two days but candy. She had no money, no destination. She didn't even know if they were traveling north or south.

So why was she laughing?

"Why are you laughing?" Brody asked from somewhere far above her. "Why are you laughing like that?"

Caitlyn lifted her head out of her hands, gasping for breath. "I don't know. There's something about poor Lyle driving around Ticaboo in his Jaguar...and here I am on the floor of your truck with a Playboy Bunny air freshener dancing in front of my nose. It just seems funny, that's all."

Lyle. So now there was a Lyle as well as a Nicky. "You'd better get up on the seat," Brody said flatly. "I think you've cut off the circulation to your head, sitting scrunched up like that."

Caitlyn was numb from her knees to her toes, and it was all she could manage to struggle onto the seat. The stinging pinpricks of sensation increased along with her circulation, and she quickly began stamping her feet on the floor, making faces and gasping with pain between the weak giggles. "That was a close call. Poor Lyle. When did we lose him?"

"Poor Lyle?" Brody shrugged, his fingers drumming a rapid staccato on the steering wheel. "A while back. He had no idea you were with me. Then again, neither did I."

"I didn't know what else to do. I saw Lyle drive up in front of the motel and I panicked. I didn't want him to see me."

Ordinarily Brody asked no questions and he told no lies, which more or less satisfied his relaxed code of honor. Until now. The curiosity he felt about Caitlyn Wilde was eating him alive, and he didn't really give a damn whether it was any of his business or not.

"Just who the hell is Lyle?" He winced inwardly, hearing the demanding bark in his voice. This was really out of character for him. It tarnished the democratic, good ol' boy image he had of himself.

She tipped her head back on the seat, taking deep breaths, her eyes shining from tears that weren't entirely from laughter. "He works for Nicky."

"And who the hell is Nicky?" he snapped. Another wince.

"If you would just calm down, I'll explain."

"I'm always calm," he said through his teeth. "Always. That's the kind of person I am—very calm, easygoing, laid back. I'm famous for being calm. I just thought you might feel you owe me some sort of explanation, that's all. But if you don't want to talk about it, then that's fine with me."

"Look, I know I owe you an explanation." She straightened her shoulders, but the uneven current in her voice hinted at tears or laughter, he wasn't sure which. "It's just that I'm not sure myself what happened. I don't even know where to begin."

"You could start with Nicky."

Caitlyn nodded, staring out the window. "He's my brother. Actually, he's my stepbrother. He's been my guardian since I was twelve years old. He owns the Las Brisas Hotel in Las Vegas. I lived there until three days ago."

Brother. Brody felt the muscles that were tied in knots slowly begin to relax. Nicky was her brother, and poor Lyle worked for Nicky. He could deal with that. "What happened three days ago?"

"Well . . . I got this craving for turkey tetrazzini." She shrugged helplessly. "That's how it all started. I had Nicky's driver take me to this little Italian restaurant on the outskirts of Vegas and told him to come back for me in an hour. I ate and I had a couple of glasses of wine—actually I think I drank most of the bottle—then I went outside to wait for the limo."

"The limo," Brody echoed. She said the word quite casually, as if she were referring to the family station wagon—which it probably was.

"Anyway, while I was waiting, I saw this bus pull up in front of the restaurant. It was full of all these tourist types wearing Bermuda shorts and T-shirts. Everybody went into the restaurant and ate, and when they got back on the bus, I just . . . got on with them. I didn't even know where it was going. I ended up touring the Grand Canyon."

She smiled faintly, shaking her head. "I'd never been there before. Those canyons were so huge and empty and breathtaking, and there wasn't a single telephone pole or smokestack or skyscraper as far as the eye could see. Every single color of the rainbow was reflected on those rocks, and the silence was so pure, so complete, that I actually heard the sound of an eagle beating its wings five hundred feet over my head. I loved the sensation of all that space around me. It was then I realized that I was alone—really alone—for the first time in my life. There were tourists around, but they didn't know me. I could do what I wanted, go where I wanted. I was absolutely drunk on freedom."

"Not to mention wine." Brody swerved the truck sharply to the right, narrowly missing a suicidal woodchuck. "Look, I understand the need to get away by yourself, but why slip out the back door? Why not pack a bag, wave goodbye and leave a forwarding address like a normal person?" He paused, thinking that last one over. "Maybe I just answered my own question."

She turned her head, throwing him a stern look. "You don't know Nicky. He would have talked me out of leaving, and he would have done it with such kindness and tact that I would have written him a thank-you note afterward. That's the way he is."

Brody pulled a package of gum from the glove box, unwrapped a piece and chomped down on it. "So what it boils down to is that you ran away from home at the tender age of . . . how old are you?"

"Twenty-two," she muttered.

"And poor Lyle is the search party." He nodded thoughtfully, but the humor in his eyes was unmistakable. "I ran away from home once. I was eleven, and my mother had made me wear blue velvet rompers to church on Easter Sunday. I can still see that outfit, right down to the white knee-high socks and that stupid clip-on bow tie. I figured I was justified."

Her eyes were becoming stinging hot again, and she knuckled them with fists. "I can't see you in blue rompers."

"I got over it," Brody said gravely. "Please, there's no need for tears on my account."

"I'm not crying. I'm just . . . a little emotional right now. Maybe it's hunger. Maybe I'm so hungry I've gone off the deep end. Brody!" Her voice suddenly rose to a shaky squeal. "Look at that!"

Startled, Brody took his foot off the accelerator, head bobbing as he scanned the road. "What? Where?"

"There!" Caitlyn pressed her nose against the window, staring with hungry eyes at a faded billboard advertising charbroiled burgers and old-fashioned shakes at Deenie's in Campcreek, twenty miles ahead. Her mouth watered. Her hollow stomach cramped, begging. "Have you ever been to Deenie's? Have you ever had a hamburger there?"

He pulled over to the side of the road and turned off the engine, staring at her with an arrested expression. "I've been to Deenie's," he said finally. "The hamburgers are all right."

"Are they worth going to jail for? I'll bet they are. I'll bet they're tender and juicy and smothered with pickles and tomatoes and lettuce, all the good stuff. I'd say that was worth going to jail for, wouldn't you?"

He passed his hand over his eyes and slumped in his seat. "What are you planning on doing, eating and running?"

"I have more class than that." She squared her shoulders, still trying to calm the weepy jumpiness inside. "After I eat, I'll surrender like a lady."

"Oh, boy." He leaned his head back on the seat and stared out the windshield. He looked as if he was making up his mind about something. After a minute he said, "I think you may be a little distressed again, Caitlyn."

"I'm completely in control," she replied with dignity. "I have a plan now. I'm going to eat, then I'm going to get arrested for not being able to pay for my food."

"Sounds foolproof." His lips twitched, but still he didn't look at her. He laced his fingers together over the top of the steering wheel. His profile was clean, pure and expressionless, cobalt-blue eyes shadowed with gold-tipped lashes. His shirt was open to mid chest, rippling gently with the sun-washed breeze. Caitlyn caught a glimpse of lovely, tough muscles and a dusky purple bruise. She swallowed involuntarily, caught off guard by an unexpected rush of feeling. For a moment, just for a moment, every part of her was stirred and warmed. She hadn't a great deal of experience with men, but intuitively she knew Brody Walker was far more complex than he would like people to believe. She found the combination of tough and tender, irreverent and reserved, so appealing that a shiver passed through her like a current.

She rolled down her window, clearing her head with a deep breath of fresh air. "I'm famous for my foolproof plans," she said, the words slightly arrhythmic. "You may have noticed."

"I noticed," he said, and there was a sigh in his voice. "All right, how about I rescue you for another hour or so? Just long enough to spring for a hamburger and maybe hear a little more about poor Lyle. My curiosity is killing me. Or is your adventurous little heart set on going to jail?"

Caitlyn hesitated, looking over her shoulder at the billboard. Food without incarceration. It was a tempting prospect, but she knew it would do her no good to continue to depend on Brody Walker. And so, with a tightly constricted throat and a great deal of regret, she said, "Thank you for the offer, but it's time I stopped inflicting myself on you."

A finger beneath her chin turned her face gently toward him. Against the window his hair was back-lit with sun, a golden halo. He gave her a slow, snake-charming smile. "Think about it," he whispered, his eyes opening very wide, very blue. "Juicy hamburgers, hot off the grill. French fries. Fresh limeade. Onion rings. Strawberry shakes, sweet and thick and creamy..."

Caitlyn murmured low in her throat. "Maybe just one more rescue," she choked out, helpless and overwhelmed. His eyes coaxed. His husky voice beguiled. She'd never been so hungry in her life, and her willpower was at an all-time low. "But only if I can pay you back when..." She paused, remembering her bleak financial outlook. When, indeed? "Actually, you may have to wait until hell freezes over," she muttered, a pained expression crossing her face. "I haven't got many prospects at the moment."

"Whenever," Brody said peacefully. "We'll just play it by ear, all right? Minute by minute. Things have a way of working out, Caitlyn."

Silence settled in the increasingly warm cab of the truck. Caitlyn tried to smile at him and failed; she tried to look away and failed at that, as well. His eyes were a mystery, bright and dark, hopeful and hopeless, young and old. Something inside her gave a tiny lurch, and the inexplicable thought came to her that Brody Walker needed rescuing just as much as she did.

Which was absurd. She didn't know him well, but he seemed tailor-made for his carefree existence, the sort of man who breezed through life on good looks and charm. She imagined there were few things a man like Brody Walker truly needed, least of all rescuing from her.

She forced a flickering smile. "On behalf of all the damsels in distress in this world, I'd like to thank you. You're bona fide hero material, Brody Walker."

His eyes grew slightly larger, shards of light spearing the dark irises. The silence that fell between them this time was so different, so utterly empty, that she knew she had unwittingly touched a nerve.

"Some people wouldn't agree with you," he said flatly. He started the truck and pulled away from the shoulder of the road in a choking cloud of dust. "We'll be in Campcreek in less than twenty minutes. You can practically smell those charbroiled burgers from here."

Brody drove automatically, his mind focused on the copper-haired woman-child sitting beside him.

He threw her sideways glances like a silent metronome, looking away each time she caught him staring.

It was then that he began to realize what was happening to him. The charisma that Caitlyn possessed, the appealing combination of sensuality and innocence, spilled through the dry, empty places in his spirit like a sparkling fountain. Each time he looked at her, the new feelings multiplied.

Brody thought he might be getting into something he wouldn't know how to get out of. If he hadn't already.

Deenie's Café rested beside a narrow, two-laned blacktop in the middle of nowhere. Campcreek made Ticaboo look like a sprawling metropolis. Most of the store windows were boarded up with plywood, and the old-fashioned Western boardwalk connecting the narrow wooden buildings was sagging and rotting away. A few of the tourist-fed businesses still had their doors open: a gas station, a hardware store and a Victorian-style motel set far back on a dusty hill that looked like something out of *Psycho*.

But Deenie's Café was a cheery vinyl and Formica oasis, filled with the aroma of sizzling beef and the sound of an old-fashioned wooden paddle fan clipping along overhead. Caitlyn's overriding impulse was to order one of everything, but she restrained herself, asking in a sweet, dignified voice for a cheeseburger and a small cola. Brody grinned at her oh-so-ladylike demeanor and ordered two hamburgers, two fresh blackberry shakes, a double order of cheese fries and two apple turnovers. Caitlyn barely resisted the urge to throw her arms around him and shower him with kisses.

They sat at a padded booth in front of a big picture window that overlooked the parking lot. Caitlyn concentrated on her food with the single-mindedness of one who didn't know where her next meal was coming from, relishing every lovely, mouth-watering morsel. Nothing, *nothing* had ever tasted so wonderful. And she knew without a doubt that nothing would ever taste so good again.

"Could I get you something else?" Brody asked, watching with amused fascination as she popped the last French fry into her mouth. He'd never seen a woman put away quite so much food in such a short amount of time. "How about a taco salad? A brown topper? Root beer float? I know, we'll order you some of those deep-fried onion curls."

"No, thank you," Caitlyn replied, lifting one eyebrow in his direction. "I don't ordinarily eat like this. I hope you realize that."

"I realize that," he said. "If you did, you wouldn't fit in the cab of my truck. I suppose you must work up a pretty good appetite, being such a fearless adventuress and all."

"A fearless adventuress?" She smiled, dampening her finger to pick up grains of salt from the French-fry basket. "No one...and I mean *no one*...

who knows me would ever describe me as a fearless adventuress.''

''How would they describe you?''

She shrugged, licking the salt off her finger. ''Color-coordinated.''

''That's it?'' He watched her lick the salt off her finger with a softly unfocused gaze. ''I know there's more to you than that.''

''Not really,'' Caitlyn said, her mouth quirking in a smile that didn't quite reach her eyes. ''I've never done anything fine or brave or noble. I've never volunteered as a candy striper at a hospital or recycled my aluminum cans or marched in a demonstration. With me, what you see is probably more than you actually get. I'm nothing special. There's no steely backbone beneath this fluffy exterior, no hidden depths to discover.''

''You really believe that?'' Brody shook his head, staring at her with incredulity. He could feel an insecurity behind the self-mocking words that seemed to pierce some unknown barrier deep in his soul. Nothing special? She could throw a hell of a temper tantrum. She was funny, resourceful, completely unpredictable. She inspired a wealth of wonderful, scary-shaky feelings with a single brilliant, whimsical smile. Even more amazing, she seemed to possess an unusual lack of awareness of her own physical appeal. He was appalled that she believed as she did, and he wondered who had given her such a low opinion of herself.

He wanted to say something reassuring and insightful that would open her eyes to her own individuality. He wanted to tell her that in his humble and expert opinion, the world would never see her like again.

But Brody was a man who lived in a man's world, and putting selfless, unvarnished emotion into words had always been difficult for him. And so, with his heart twisting in all kinds of directions and an odd huskiness in his voice, he said, "You have some catsup on your chin."

She picked up her napkin. "Where?"

"Here." He leaned over the table and touched the spot on her chin. Then, before she could move, before he could think of a dozen manly reasons not to put his heart out on his sleeve, he said softly, "You're special, Caitlyn Wilde. So special, I'm in real danger of making a fool of myself over you."

She forgot the catsup. Her eyes opened wide, focusing on the beautiful, oddly vulnerable lines of his mouth. The napkin fluttered to the table, but her hand remained poised in midair. A stinging heat spilled within her, all through her, waking her up with a jewel-like clarity.

"I'll meet you halfway," Brody whispered.

They leaned forward in identical, hesitant slow motion. Brody's heart was in his throat, as if he was playing some grand romantic love scene instead of stealing a kiss over a cluttered table at Deenie's Café.

It seemed to take forever before his lips touched hers, so lightly, yet he shivered clear through to his soul. He pulled back slightly, because this need, this helplessness was new to him, and he had to know if she felt it, too. Her eyes opened slowly, dark and feverish. Her mouth parted on a soft breath, then curved in a faint, disbelieving smile that matched his own. His mouth closed over hers once again in a sleepy, lazy kiss so long and deep he could have lost himself in it. His hands clasped the edges of the table in a white-knuckled grip. His body yearned for more.

When he finally pulled back, his chest moved in shallow, rapid inhalations. He stared at Caitlyn numbly. Her wondering eyes captured him, held him motionless. He had the sensation that the world had drifted far, far away, and all the old demons were trembling at their sudden lack of significance.

"I don't know what to say," he whispered.

Caitlyn felt a wild pulse thumping in her throat. He was so charming to her, with a heat stain on the handsome line of his cheekbone and the oddly defenseless expression in his eyes. His broad shoulders were curved in a relaxed, careless posture she knew was a lie.

Flushing everywhere with a deep, penetrating warmth, she turned her head toward the window. This must be what was known as an awkward moment, she thought, the quiet after the impulse. Lost in her thoughts, it took her a moment to notice the billowing cloud of dust in the parking lot. Another car had pulled in, a low-slung black Jaguar with Nevada license plates.

Feeling like the sky had suddenly landed on the top of her head, she said quietly, "Oh, boy..."

Brody's head swiveled, following the direction of her gaze. He drew in a sharp breath, eyes narrowed. "That guy is really starting to irritate me."

They looked at each other, then at Lyle as he climbed out of the car. His hands were waving in front of his face, trying to clear the dust from the air.

"Doesn't look like he's in much of a hurry," Brody said.

"He probably just stopped to eat. He had no idea he's about to earn a four-figure Christmas bonus."

"I always figured a man ought to work for his money." Brody pulled a twenty-dollar bill out of his pocket and tossed it onto the table. "How do you feel about back doors?"

Four

Caitlyn had never been involved in a high-speed chase, but running from Lyle Switzer gave her just a hint of what she had been missing all these years.

They crept around the outside of the building, keeping low. Brody had actually whispered the words, "Keep low," then he had grinned at Caitlyn as if he was enjoying thwarting Lyle just as much as she was. Feeling like a character in a spy movie, Caitlyn had scrambled right behind her leader, one hand clinging to his leather belt. Once she raised her head just enough to catch a glimpse of Lyle through the window. He had a snowy white napkin tucked into the collar of his shirt and was digging into a piece of pie with great gusto. She started to snicker and Brody pulled her right down again, telling her to behave. They weren't out of the woods yet.

Fortunately Brody had parked his truck on the east side of the building, taking advantage of the shade offered by a cottonwood tree. The only window was effectively screened by a big blue dumpster. It was nothing at all to scramble in the truck and zip down a dusty side road rather than risk turning onto the main highway, where Lyle could spot them. They had no idea where they were headed, and they didn't care. The important thing was that Lyle Switzer would not be getting his Christmas bonus this year.

With their tires spitting gravel and a trail of dust behind them, they bounced along the rutted road at a thrilling pace. Caitlyn was laughing as though she wouldn't quit in the near future. Brody was twisting all over the seat, looking out the rear window for signs of the black Jaguar, looking out the front window to try to anticipate the next ditch they would be hurdling.

"It doesn't take much to amuse you, does it?" Brody commented, watching his passenger clutch her middle and slip farther and farther down in the seat. "You're going to get a stitch in your side if you keep it up."

"I don't care." And she didn't. At the moment, she felt wonderfully, divinely detached from reality. She was no longer concerned with the future. She felt reckless, lighthearted and completely divorced from responsibility. "I can't remember the last time my life was so interesting. Do you think Lyle will follow us?''

"I doubt it." Brody grinned as they skidded around a narrow curve. "I'm just driving like a bat out of hell because you seem to enjoy it so much."

Caitlyn wiped her streaming eyes with the cuff of her shirt. "Thank you. That's very thoughtful. Las Vegas was never this much fun."

"Now that's a little hard to believe, city girl." Brody negotiated a narrow wooden bridge at freeway speed. "Las Vegas is not exactly a sleepy, one-horse town."

"That depends on your perspective," Caitlyn replied. "Nicky wanted me to feel needed so he always made sure I was busy—playing hostess when he entertained, ordering fresh flowers for the restaurant, picking out new fabric for the umbrellas around the pool area . . . that kind of thing. I spent my time taking care of a great many unimportant details and that sort of life can be monotonous regardless of where you live."

Conversation ceased as they came upon a flock of sheep ambling down the middle of the road. Brody kept his hand on the horn as he tried to negotiate the woolly obstacle course, but the sheep were unimpressed. Finally he stopped the truck, giving Caitlyn an apologetic shrug. "One of the drawbacks of country driving . . . sheep traffic jams. We'll have to wait it out."

"I don't mind." Caitlyn dropped her head against the seat, still smiling. "In fact, I've never been more content in my life, which is strange, considering I don't even know where we are."

"We're pretty much lost," Brody said calmly. "You, me and the sheep. Still, look on the bright side. Poor Lyle can't possibly find us if we don't even know where we are."

"I don't mind being lost. It's much better than being found."

"Now all we have to do is stay lost until Lyle has enough time to leave Campcreek. Then we back-track along this road, and voilà—we're not lost anymore." Brody winked at her, the corners of his mouth curling upward. "Don't thank me, ma'am. This hero business just comes naturally to me."

"All this and he's modest, too." She turned her head and smiled at him. It started out innocently enough, just a shared smile. But somewhere along the way the comfortable camaraderie disappeared, replaced by startling, hungry feelings that she could almost see. That kiss was there between them, and all the stinging anticipation it had aroused. She could see the stark need in his eyes as they drifted slowly to her lips. His mouth tightened, as if he were in some sort of pain. Knowing she was capable of unnerving this experienced, infinitely appealing man filled her with an unfamiliar, primitive excitement. She had never tested her sexuality before. Her one and only intimate experience had been accomplished with a great lack of finesse in the back of a Volkswagen bus in high school. It had been an act of rebellion against Nicky's china-doll treatment rather than an act of passion. She had regretted it ever since. She couldn't forget the empty, powerless feelings she had had when all was said and done and the fantasy had turned to a sticky, embarrassed reality.

But now...she had a taste of what it might be like to influence Brody Walker. To arouse him, to make him wait and wonder and *want* her. It was intoxicating, and a soft heat filled her body as she stared at him through a heavy veil of lashes.

He didn't look like someone Caitlyn Wilde could affect. He looked like a man who had seen and done it all and been impressed by very little. A man who might share laughter with others, but who would never share his pain. A man who kept his secrets. What was it about an isolated spirit that women found so irresistible?

Her heartbeat spilled into her throat as she moistened her dry lips with her tongue. She didn't move a muscle, yet her body seemed to be flowing toward him.

"You're out of your depth," Brody said softly, as if he'd read her mind. "Fair warning."

A challenge? She managed to smile, even though she felt a shudder of excitement take her. "I'm not worried. I can take care of—"

"Yourself. I know." Such a reckless little girl. He knew she was testing him, just as he knew he could probably have her if he made the moves that came so easily to him. She had absolutely no idea what she was flirting with. This was an adventure to her, a long-awaited chance to try her wings. Looking at her now, he saw the undefended youth and innocence that helped him check the yearning that was eating him alive. He turned his head away from her and the entrancing picture she made: the lazy breeze tugging a strand of burnished hair across her parted lips, a world of questions in her dark eyes. Questions he knew all the answers to, Lord help them both.

Naive, pretty and vulnerable, he thought grimly. His attraction to her was an unrelenting force, one that was fighting his will to deny it. He was crazy to encourage Caitlyn's dependency on him. He knew he had the power to harm her, and it would be in her best interest if he severed their relationship now. He also knew he wasn't going to. She had touched a place inside him that was desperately needy, and he wanted more. He couldn't explain it, he couldn't justify it. He knew only that the story was far from over, and all the old rules no longer applied.

She was so innocent and trusting that his conscience prodded him to improve her odds against him. "You don't want to play this game with me," he said quietly. "I'm not sure how experienced you are, and I'm likely to cheat."

Caitlyn stared straight ahead at nothing, feeling like she had been slapped in the face. She drew an unsatisfying breath, and when she spoke, the words came too fast. "I'm not playing games. I don't know what you're talking about."

"Don't you?"

She flicked him a sideways glance, lifting her chin fractionally. "No."

"Would you like a demonstration?" His voice had dropped to a silky drawl. His smile could have broken hearts, and the sexual heat in his gaze was frank and undisguised. He lifted his hand, rolling the center button on her blouse between his thumb and forefinger. Then, ever so slowly, his hand skimmed sideways, fingertips grazing her nipple with an agonizing, delicate pressure. Watching her face with a heavy-lidded intensity, he drew soft, tingling circles that held her still and quiet and breathless. "There are games and there are games, Caitlyn. Be damn sure of what you're getting into before you close your eyes and jump."

Her eyes *were* closed, Caitlyn realized with a guilty flush. She opened them, trying to clear her distracted thoughts. One touch and he practically burned the soles off her shoes. What on earth had made her think she was a match for a man like Brody Walker? Sweet Caitlyn Wilde, who had feigned stomach flu in high school for the entire two weeks her health class studied sex education. "Is the demonstration over?" she asked faintly.

Brody nodded and folded his hands in his lap like a good boy. "Yes, ma'am."

"Fine. I'll just sit here and hyperventilate for a while, then."

Brody grinned at her. Her head was bent, fluffy bangs tangled over her forehead, a glossy curtain of sun-washed hair falling forward to hide her face. He could barely see the tip of her little nose. "Don't get me wrong. I think you're one in a million. You make it almost impossible for me to remember my hero responsibilities."

Caitlyn turned her head, her brown eyes holding fast to his. "Brody? Can I ask you something?"

He sensed trouble coming. He could tell by her voice that this was one of those emotional, woman-type questions that made a man clear his throat and wish he were in Timbuktu. "As long as you don't ask me how to spell anything," he replied uneasily.

"You've had a lot experience, right? I mean ... with women?"

He sighed and passed his hand over his eyes. "On second thought, why don't you ask me how to spell something?"

"I was just wondering how you saw me," she said with difficulty. "Would you say I was fairly repressed and conservative? Or would you say I had possibilities?"

He stared at her. "Pardon me?"

She colored but decided to persevere. After all, it wasn't like he didn't already know she was an idiot. "Do you think I'm different from other women you've known?"

That one was easy. "Oh, yes."

"I guess that answers my question, doesn't it?" Her sigh was melancholy. "The sparrow can fly from the nest, but she's still a sparrow."

"How poetic," Brody said. "And how absolutely stupid." He brought his hand from his lap to brush his fingers over her lips. He could feel the uncertainty in her eyes reaching out to him, and the impulse to drag her into his arms nearly overcame him. He forced a smile, though the tense muscles in his jaw protested.

"Somewhere beneath that color-coordinated exterior of yours is a free-spirited Gypsy just waiting to show herself. She already has the power to stop my heart with a smile. Lord help me when she gets a little experience." His hand moved to her cheek, his thumb sculpting the lovely rise of her cheekbone. "You're just beginning, Caitlyn Wilde. There's so much for you to see and learn and discover about yourself...don't let your doubts hold you back. You can do anything you want to do, be anything you want to be."

Her smile was soft with disbelief. "I don't know where to begin. I really don't."

With me, he thought, feeling fiercely, overwhelmingly male. But he hadn't lost all reason yet, and he knew she had to stand on her own two feet if she was ever going to believe in herself. "You've got a whole world of choices," he said, deliberately pulling back his hand. "You just need to make them."

Feeling oddly bereft without his touch, Caitlyn turned her head and stared out the window. She touched the diamond studs in her ears, nervously twisting them in her fingers. What to do now? She had a field of daisies on her right, a flock of sheep on her left and an empty sky above. Her assets were limited to the clothes on her back, the sandals falling off her feet and her earrings. She thought it was rather optimistic of Brody to say that she had a world of choices.

"I could go back," she said almost inaudibly.

"It's your decision." He sounded distant.

"Or I could hop out of the truck right here and live off the land," she went on gloomily. "Eat nuts and berries and make little traps for varmints."

"Varmints?" Brody echoed, a glimmer of amusement in his voice. "Oh, now she's cooking."

Caitlyn went back to fiddling with her earrings. "Well, the way I see it, I'm stuck between a rock and a..."

Rock, she thought suddenly. Rock. Stone. *Diamond*. She had diamonds in her ears—dazzling, glorious, blue-white diamonds that were worth a small fortune.

"I'm dying of suspense," Brody said. "Caught between a rock and a what?"

"A pawnshop."

He digested this thoughtfully. "You're caught between a rock and a pawnshop?"

She looked at him impatiently. "No! I *need* a pawnshop. I can pawn these—" she tugged on her earrings "—and get enough money to tide me over for weeks. I'll have time to find a job, a place to live, money to buy clothes...all I need to do is go back to Campcreek and find a pawnshop—"

"I don't want to rain on your parade," Brody interrupted, "but there isn't a pawnshop in Campcreek."

Caitlyn shrugged. She wasn't about to be deterred at this point, not when her ingenuity was finally showing signs of life. "All right. I'll go back to Campcreek and hitch a ride to the next town. We can't be that far from civilization."

He nodded thoughtfully, his body twisted slightly in the seat to face her. "Not a bad idea. You know, something else just occurred to me. Moab can't be too far away from here."

"What's Moab?"

"It's a town in southern Utah, close to the Arizona border. It's a good-size place, a stopover for tourists who enjoy climbing and backpacking through all that red-rock scenery you liked so well in the Grand Canyon. I'm sure there would be a pawnshop there, not to mention a decent motel." He grinned slowly, his eyes reflecting the bright blue of the summer sky. "Matter of fact, it just so happens I'm headed there myself."

"You are?" Caitlyn floundered, falling victim to the sensual impact of that smile. "You're serious, you're really going . . ." She couldn't remember the name of the town. She couldn't remember her own name.

"Moab." Eyes dancing, he clapped her on the shoulder in a companionable gesture. "I'm entered in the Canyonlands Rodeo there tomorrow night. Isn't this a fortuitous coincidence? You can hitch a ride with me."

Caitlyn fell in love with Moab, a picturesque town in the heart of Utah's canyon country. It reminded her of a cross between Taos and Aspen, and the surrounding red-rock landscape was stark, primitive and gloriously limitless. The people she glimpsed on the sidewalks of the main thoroughfare were a fascinating blend of hippies, tourists, miners and cowboys. Everyone seemed to move at the same easygoing pace, whether they were in cars, on mountain bikes or on foot.

While Brody checked into the motel, Caitlyn walked across the street to the Indian Trading Post and Pawnshop. Five minutes later she had two thousand dollars in her pocket and a satisfied smile on her face. The pawnbroker had initially offered her one-third that amount, and she had immediately set her lower lip to quivering. It had been a wonderful performance and had saved her a great deal of haggling.

She wandered through the store, looking at the variety of casual Western clothing, leather goods and

Indian jewelry. Smoothing her hand over baby-soft, form-fitting jeans, she felt like an imposter. Caitlyn Wilde didn't wear clothes like this. She wore designer labels and Italian pumps and all the proper undergarments. She wore a bra like she wore a seat belt in a car, strapping herself firmly in for protection. Her breasts never bounced. Her panty line never showed. The breeze had never dared to toss her skirt around her hips. She walked carefully, chose her words carefully, made sure to stay quietly in the background with a smile on her face. Nicky was the powerhouse in the family. He made all the decisions and took all the risks, and there was nothing he liked better than winning on a long shot. He seemed to thrive on the excitement, attention and uncertainty he so zealously guarded Caitlyn from. Caitlyn hadn't a worry in the world with Nicky in charge, and that gave her security, safety... and restlessness.

She picked up a pair of cloud-bleached jeans at random and saw they were a size smaller than she usually wore. It would probably take her thirty minutes to pour herself into them. Half the women in the store were wearing the same skin-tight jeans, some with clingy tank tops, some with faded T-shirts. Very few seemed to be wearing bras, makeup or jewelry, and they all looked delightfully unencumbered.

Caitlyn bought two pairs of jeans, leather thongs and a beaded Indian belt that was on sale for $2.99. Her adrenaline started to pump, and her smile felt like it was becoming quite permanent. She went next door to Jeremiah's Emporium and purchased a black denim skirt, a man's white cotton shirt, hiking shorts, a couple of T-shirts and an economy-size package of bikini briefs. She didn't buy a nightgown. She didn't buy nylons or heels, and she didn't buy a bra. She felt absolutely reckless for the first time in her life, and it was a *wonderful* feeling. Her last stop on the way to the motel was at a drugstore. She bought a few personal items, a cheap blow dryer and a child-size overnight bag in fluorescent stripes.

Brody's truck wasn't parked in front of the motel when she returned, and Caitlyn remembered him saying something about registering for the rodeo. She was more than happy to have a little time to herself. She had a miracle to perform, and miracles took a little time when you were just a beginner.

She showered, then put on the nylon underpants and used the blow dryer to fluff her hair into careless disarray. She felt wonderfully, utterly uninhibited standing in the steamy bathroom wearing nothing but bikini underpants and a smile. Her skin was tanned to a golden bronze, her stomach was smooth and flat, and her breasts were heavy with a pleasant, tender weight. She closed her eyes and turned her head from side to side, feeling her hair brush like warm velvet on her bare shoulders. Her smile grew wider. It didn't matter in the least that there was no man to appreciate this gloriously feminine creature. For the first time in her life she was appreciating herself.

She executed several energetic pirouettes into the bedroom and turned on the radio on the bedside table. Some rock star was crooning about the pretty woman who'd stolen his heart. The song fit her liberated mood beautifully. She pulled a pillow off the bed and did a few turns around the room with her soft, fluffy partner. She *felt* pretty, prettier than designer clothes and silk stockings had ever made her feel. Nude dancing in an ecomony-priced motel room. Whatever would Caitlyn Wilde do next?

She would get dressed, Caitlyn decided, shivering in her chicken-skinned flesh. Dancing in the nude was very liberating, but it did have its drawbacks. She put on the denim miniskirt and white cotton shirt, then rolled up the cuffs and left four buttons undone. She knotted the shirt at the waist, leaving a narrow strip of skin above the waistband of the skirt. She may have been wearing a man's shirt, but she felt all woman. She had a suspicion that part of that feeling was connected to the underwire bra dangling over the rim of the wastebasket.

There was no powdering her nose for a finishing touch, since she had neglected to buy any makeup. Her face would shine and her freckles would stand out, and that was all good and fine. She had discovered something very reassuring about herself in the past forty-eight hours. When her back was against the wall and the chips were stacked against her, she was actually quite resilient. She looked at herself in the mirror, and her smile turned to a laugh. Well, the

last remnants of a spoiled society baby were gone.
The fresh-faced young woman staring back at her
was like an empty canvas, ready for colors, shapes
and texture. Ready for anything.

Brody thought he might be having a heart attack.

He'd been feeling just dandy until he'd walked
past Caitlyn's motel room and heard the music. Hell,
the whole town of Moab could hear the music, she
had it turned up so loud. It surprised him, since he'd
pegged her as the easy-listening, symphony-on-
Saturday-night type. He hardly expected to find her
rattling the windows in their frames with good old
fashioned rock and roll.

Naturally he paused outside her window. He was
curious, and the drapes were pulled just enough for
a very narrow peephole. Since a kindly fate had pro-
vided the means, he peeped.

His visibility was limited to the foot of the bed and
a small mountain of paper bags piled on the carpet
nearby. And then he blinked, and he asked himself
if he had just seen a naked woman twirl past the
window. His heart began to palpitate, slamming
painfully against his tender ribs.

Wishful thinking, Brody thought, pressing his fists
into his eyes. But when he looked again, the vision
had reappeared.

Caitlyn's back was to the window, and she was
cuddling a fat, fluffy pillow and dancing with great

enthusiasm. She wasn't *quite* naked, as he had orig-
inally thought. She was wearing white bikini briefs
that molded her sweet curves with heart-stopping
attention to detail. Her flame-dark hair was flying as
she turned and swayed with that lucky, lucky pillow
clutched to her breasts. She danced out of view and
he sighed softly; she danced back in again and his
heart doubled its hectic rhythm. He began to per-
spire.

He loved the slight indentation of her spine as it
dipped through the small of her back. He loved her
long, bare legs, the child-size span of her waist, the
sun-kissed glow of her skin. She looked carefree,
uninhibited and incredibly sexy, and Brody felt a
powerful and disturbing combination of pleasure
and pain. He wanted her. He wanted her with an intensity that truly frightened him, because fierce
emotion wasn't part of his character. Not any longer.

"Caitlyn," he whispered, hearing the sound of her
name deep in the aching silence of his spirit.

He turned away from the window, and suddenly
the water-color sunset felt painfully bright to his
eyes. He felt panic shivering through his veins as he
considered for the first time in years the possibility
that he might actually find himself needing someone. And even more frightening, the possibility that
someone might need him.

His senses felt numb and lifeless as he walked to
his room next door, though he was still aware of the
unrelenting need within him. He took a much-needed

cold shower, then stretched out on the bed with his arms hooked behind his neck. He was dripping wet and naked as the day he was born, but the air-conditioning blasting from the overhead vents did nothing to cool the fire in his blood. Lord, he was hot.

Just a few feet away from him, alone in her motel room, was a born-again Gypsy who was more than ready to come out and play. She was waiting for a man to sweep her up in his arms and teach her about life and passion. After a lifetime of repression, she was aching to be taught, aching to know everything there was to know. If not Brody, then someone else would inevitably find his way into her bed and her heart. Just knowing that made him half-crazy inside, torn in a dozen different directions. *Caitlyn, Caitlyn...*

Brody closed his eyes, feeling the black devils that visited him every so often take him by the throat. It happened every time he started thinking there might be something more for him in this life than a hell of a mediocre good time. Something worth fighting for, something that would give him one more shot at being an honest-to-goodness hero.

You had your chance, Brody. And you pretty much showed God and everybody just what you were made of, didn't you?

He jumped up from the bed and dressed in jeans and a denim shirt. He was going down to the Sweet Alice bar and get good and drunk. And then he would cuddle up with the first sweet young thing who batted her eyelashes at him, a friend till death or until sunrise, whichever came first. He would have a fine time. A *damn* fine time.

He stomped out the door, then slammed it behind him.

Five

Caitlyn wasn't sure when Brody returned to the motel, but she knew exactly when he left again. He slammed his door with enough force to shake the walls between them, then clomped right past her room. The sound of cowboy boots on the redwood porch was unmistakable.

She ran to the window just in time to watch Brody climb into his truck and drive away. He wore a fresh blue shirt, and his curly hair looked almost tame. She couldn't see his face clearly, but something about the impatient way he moved suggested serious carousing ahead.

Caitlyn sat down on the edge of the bed, feeling like all the bubbles in her champagne had gone flat, her balloon had been popped and the sun had gone behind a cloud all at once. Here she was, all dressed down for the first time in years, and nowhere to go. No one to impress with her shiny nose and ordinary clothes. All the blue-eyed cowboys were out for the evening.

Well, she would be darned—no, *damned*—if she was going to sit around a lonely motel room all night long feeling sorry for herself. It wasn't like she'd been seduced and abandoned by some heinous villain. Brody had seen her safely to Moab, just as he'd promised. He probably figured he had more than fulfilled his guardian angel responsibilities and that it was finally time to cut loose. More than likely he would spend the entire night womanizing from one end of the town to the other.

A stab of hurt twisted sharp and deep as memories collected in her mind like hazy postcards... Brody standing in the rain with his hair plastered to his head...the smile that began in his bright blue eyes and spread to his lips...a quiet moment at Deenie's when he whispered, "I'll meet you halfway...."

Of course it hadn't meant anything to him. It was purely a natural response with Brody. He was a charming, wisecracking expert on good times and fast moves. He wasn't about to change his ways just because Caitlyn Wilde was getting her little heart bruised.

Well, two could play this game. She was just as capable of, if not quite as experienced at, drinking from the cup of life as Brody Walker. She stuffed her room key and a fifty-dollar bill into her pocket, then hid the rest of her cash beneath the mattress. Her breathing was quick and shallow as she headed out the door, short skirt brushing her thighs, bare breasts tingling against the light cotton fabric of her shirt. She'd lost a little of her spunk, but none of her determination. She was young, she was healthy and she was free. There was nothing on earth to stop her from finally raising a little hell.

Brody was dog-paddling in self-pity. The evening wasn't turning out the way he'd planned. His spirits were as flat as his warm beer, and some jackass kept playing old Beach Boys songs on the jukebox. Brody was in no mood for the Beach Boys. Hell, when he was in the heart of Utah's desert country, he wanted to hear old country songs or maybe Lacy J. Dalton. Anything but those damned surfing songs.

A cute little brunette at the bar tried to catch his eye and he quickly looked away, hunching over his beer. It wasn't his usual style, sitting alone in a dark corner away from all the action. Then again, he didn't feel like his usual self tonight. He felt like a stranger he was meeting for the first time, and he was almost afraid to find out what he was going to do next. Every second held a nerve-racking anticipation.

He couldn't get Caitlyn out of his mind, and he couldn't stop his mind from playing nasty tricks on his body. Primitive urges burned deep within him, pitiless and constant. He wanted nothing more than to walk out of the Sweet Alice bar and head straight to the motel. But if he did that, if he saw her again while he was in this pathetic condition, he knew he would forget all the good reasons for keeping his distance. He'd grown a pretty tough shell over the years, but now, when he needed it most, it was cracking and peeling like old paint. Lord only knew what he would find underneath.

"If your head sinks any lower, you could blow bubbles in that beer with your nose."

Brody grinned for the first time that night, recognizing the feisty bass voice of Lonnie Ray Arnold. He stood up, holding out his hand to the heavily muscled bear of a man standing across the table. "I thought you were dead, Lonnie Ray. Somebody told me you'd entered the wild cow milking in Waco and got yourself kicked in the head."

Brown leathery skin folded and crinkled around Lonnie Ray's smile. He was forty and looked sixty, thanks to a lifetime in the sun and a shaggy mane of silver hair. "Funny about that," he said. "I heard pretty much the same thing about you. Some big nasty quarter horse walked all over you at a rodeo in Pinetop. Ain't it a shame how embarrassing stories like that get around?"

Brody chuckled and pulled out a chair for his friend. "Sit down and change the subject, Lonnie Ray. I don't care to discuss the rodeo in Pinetop."

Lonnie Ray pulled up a chair and took a swig from Brody's beer. "Well, you weren't drinking it," he said when Brody gave him a questioning look. "You were crying in it, but you weren't drinking it. You got yourself a sad story you want to tell me?"

Brody had met Lonnie Ray at a rodeo in Jackson Hole fifteen years earlier. Everyone who knew anything about rodeoing knew about Lonnie Ray Arnold. In his younger days he had been a champion bull rider and the National Rodeo Association's All-Around Cowboy three years running. An accident with a mean-spirited Brahma had left him with twenty-seven broken bones, one less kidney and a strong desire to make a career adjustment. Rather than leave the rodeo circuit altogether, he started the Bar-A Stock Company, now one of the major stock contractors for the National Rodeo Association. He was also one of Brody's few close friends, despite his irritating habit of seeing too much.

"No sad stories here," Brody muttered, signaling to the waitress to bring him another beer. "I'm just enjoying a little solitude, getting geared up for the rodeo tomorrow."

"As I recall, you usually had a different method of gearing yourself up for a rodeo." Lonnie Ray nodded at the giggling brunette at the bar who was doing everything but handstands to get Brody's attention. "And it didn't have a damn thing to do with solitude."

"Can't a man sit and enjoy a drink by himself? Maybe I don't feel like exerting myself tonight. Maybe I want to sit here and meditate about life and death and taxes. Had you thought of that, Lonnie Ray?"

"Can't say I had." Lonnie Ray controlled himself as long as he could, then threw his silvery head back and gave a rumbling belly laugh. "I can't wait to see her, Brody. She must be something."

"Who?" Brody really wanted another beer. Where was that waitress?

"The woman who has you roped and tied like a poor little calf. It's written all over your face, Brody."

Brody lost a good ten seconds before he could come up with an answer. "You're getting senile, Lonnie Ray. You'd better hightail it home to Wyoming and take up whittling."

"I have to say, I never thought I'd see the day. You've been keeping yourself pretty free and easy since everything that happened with Jenny. It's good to see you finally—"

"I don't want to talk about Jenny," Brody said. His voice was soft, slightly hoarse. "That's ancient history."

A pause. "Not as long as you carry it around with you, it's not. You're not to blame for what happened."

"Maybe I'll head over to the Whistle Pig next door. At least they bring you a beer the same day you order it."

Lonnie Ray held up his big callused hands in a gesture of surrender. "All right, don't go off in a huff. I'm sorry. I'll leave you to screw up your life all by your little lonesome. Damn, what's going on with the music around here?"

"That's the Beach Boys," Brody muttered.

"Good ol' Willie sure could teach them a thing or two."

The waitress finally brought Brody's beer, and he raised it in a toast. "Here's to Willie Nelson," he said, clicking his glass against Lonnie Ray's. "May he live forever. And—" He stopped abruptly, feeling like he'd been hit across the chest with a plank as he saw the threesome entering the bar. Two laughing, clean-shaven cowboys, a good ten years younger than Brody and each sporting a brand new Stetson. And with them, cuddled right between them like she belonged there, was Caitlyn Wilde. She had on a man's shirt, unbuttoned to heart-attack level, and a short denim skirt that showed off her bare legs. Her smile was dazzling, without a doubt the strongest source of light in the room.

"Oh, hell," Brody muttered, feeling the knot in his belly twist a little tighter.

Lonnie Ray perked right up. "'Oh, hell' what?" His gaze lit on Caitlyn and he whistled softly. "Well, powder my butt and call me a jelly doughnut... what have we here?''

Brody's mouth thinned. "Two men and a baby."

"She doesn't look much like a baby to me," Lonnie Ray replied thoughtfully. "There's something about that smile of hers, like she knows every itch a man could have and right where to scratch it."

"She barely knows how to tie her shoes," Brody snapped. He knew he wasn't being fair, but he was filled with a blind, unreasoning anger. All night long he'd been visualizing Caitlyn sitting alone in her motel room, watching Johnny Carson on television and now and then peeking out the window to see if Brody had returned yet. Thinking about him. Longing for him, the way he'd been longing for her. What the hell was she doing having a good time? "She's the last person I expected to see here tonight."

"Is she a particular friend of yours?"

"From what I can see, she isn't *particular* at all." Brody's eyes narrowed as he watched Caitlyn and her new friends take a table in the far corner. "I don't believe this. She has absolutely no business spending time with a couple of losers like that."

"You know them, then?" Lonnie Ray asked calmly.

"I know their type," Brody replied. He had to concentrate on unclenching his jaw before he cracked a couple of molars. "Shiftless. Good-for-nothing. Give 'em an inch and they take a mile, especially where a woman is concerned."

"Well, let me put your mind at ease," Lonnie Ray said cheerfully. "Those two boys—they happen to be brothers, name of Marty and Keith Finch—well, those two work for me, looking after the stock. They come from a good churchgoing family, they're hard workers and highly principled. Your friend there is in good hands."

Hands, Brody thought, quickly looking to see where those highly principled boys were putting their hands. Finch number one was behaving himself, hands clasped on the tabletop. Finch number two was getting a little frisky, his arm draped over the back of Caitlyn's chair. He was leaning too close, as well, and laughing too much. He had too many teeth. For her part, Caitlyn seemed to be having a grand old time, dark eyes filled with spice and excitement, hands gesturing this way and that way as she spoke. Her legs were crossed at the ankle, the denim skirt riding high on her slender thighs. The dusty overhead light picked out the delicate strands of red and gold in her hair. She was luminous.

"I half suspect she's gotten herself drunk," Brody muttered, noting the unusually high color in her cheeks.

Lonnie Ray's eyebrows raised halfway up his forehead. "Drunk? Now what on earth makes you say a thing like that?"

"Just the way she's acting."

"Oh. You mean laughing, talking, stuff like that?"

Brody glared at him. "I do hope you're having a good time, Lonnie Ray. I just live to amuse you."

The older man laughed. "And tonight you're doing a fine job of it. I've seen women scratch and hiss like cats over you, but I've never seen you bristle up like this over any woman. It's refreshing, it really is. I figured you were pretty much immune to that green-eyed monster."

"What? Do you think I'm jealous?" Brody shook his head, his gaze sliding back to that corner table. Finch number one didn't have his hands on top of the table any longer. They were somewhere under the table, and Brody didn't like that one bit. "I'm not the type. I just don't like to see a woman taken advantage of, that's all, especially a friend. Caitlyn's obviously got herself in a bad situation there."

"On account of being fried to her tonsils?" Lonnie Ray asked innocently.

"Well, there's one sure way to find out," Brody growled. He stood up, kicking his chair back. His eyes were riveted on Caitlyn as he stalked across the room, his brows drawn together, his emotions darker than a thundercloud. He came up behind her and leaned over to whisper in her ear.

"Boo," he said.

Caitlyn yelped and knocked over her drink. Finch number one got himself soaked from the belt buckle down, and quickly excused himself to clean up in the rest room. Finch number two tried to mop up the mess with a tiny cocktail napkin.

"Thank you very much, Brody," Caitlyn said, tossing her hair so it slapped him in the face. "Your manners are perfectly exquisite. How utterly delightful to see you."

Not drunk, Brody decided, looking at the clear blaze of anger in her dark eyes. She was using too many big words and pronouncing them too well.

He closed his eyes briefly, counting to ten. It was always good to count to ten before you did something dangerous and irrational. "Caitlyn?"

"What?" Her voice was mutinous, her expression guarded.

"Dance with me." It was there in his voice, all the longing, all the need he had been fighting since he'd met her. And the surrender.

Caitlyn opened her mouth to refuse, then closed it again. "Oh, Lord," she whispered, holding Brody's eyes. She felt like she was poised on the edge of a cliff, waiting to see if she would fly or fall when she jumped. Heaven or hell on the toss of a coin...

"Please," he said, holding out his hand. He couldn't remember the last time he'd said "please" to a woman. He knew he'd go down on his knees and beg just to hold her close to him.

She stood up and took his hand. She thought she heard a sound behind her, a protest from her new young friend whose name she couldn't remember. It didn't matter. For this moment, Brody was the center of her universe, and going into his arms was like coming home. Her hips went slowly against his, nestling warmly in the cradle of his thighs. Her hand slipped behind his neck, and her face nestled against his chest. She couldn't have said whether the music playing was soft or fast, sweet or low. The heartbeat beneath her cheek was her rhythm. She closed her eyes, imagining everyone else in the room slipping away until they were alone in the smoky dimness. Barely moving, barely breathing. She'd never felt anything so perfect as this moment, anything so right.

"You feel so good," Brody whispered huskily. His lips brushed the top of her head, and he drew her closer against him. "So small...I could put you in my pocket and keep you forever."

Caitlyn smiled against his shoulder. "Do you know what I wanted to do tonight?"

"What?"

"Raise hell."

Brody's chest lifted with a hard sigh. Somewhere along the way, their dance had become an embrace. Their feet were barely moving. Their bodies were straining together, and the warmth they shared was quickly becoming a scorching heat. Deliberately he moved his hips against her, letting her feel his arousal.

"You're raising hell, sweetheart," he said. He stopped moving altogether, pulling back just far enough to look into her eyes. There wasn't a flicker of amusement in his expression. "I wonder if you realize that?"

His hands slipped over her shoulders, moved slowly down her arms and came to rest on either side of her hips. Caitlyn softened helplessly against him, a rare and stinging warmth flooding deep inside her. Certain muscles tightened painfully, others grew moist and tender with an aching need. And it was all happening too fast, she could hardly take it in.

"Is that a warning?" she whispered hoarsely, her hands working convulsively on his shoulders.

"Probably the only one you're going to get." He continued to gaze into her eyes with a dark, fierce gravity. Every nerve ending in his body was fraying. He could take her hand and walk out of here with her now. There was a blanket of stars waiting for them outside. Still, he was torn with conflicting emotions, tenderness and fear and desire all fighting for control.

"I'm a big girl, Brody. I can take care of—"

She never had a chance to finish the sentence. Suddenly he had her by the arm and was steering her across the wooden dance floor. His grip was tight, almost painful, and the expression on his face was grim. He pulled her outside, down the front steps and around the corner of the building where an army of cats yowled and scattered.

"Take care of *me*," Brody whispered fiercely, his hands closing over her shoulders.

And then he had her in his arms in a seizure of need, his fingers plowing into her hair, his hips grinding against hers. He had stopped courting her innocence. Hurting her was the last thing he wanted to do, but he was too desperate to be gentle. He'd been alone so long. It was a feeling that had never left him, whether he shared his bed or slept alone. Until now.

His tongue mated with hers, riding liquid fire in deep, hungry strokes. His knee thrust between her thighs, his hands making yearning motions on the small of her back, then lower, to cup the softness of her bottom and lift her slightly off the ground. He shuddered with arousal, every fiber of his being reaching out to her. And she welcomed him.

A truck turned into the parking lot, horn blasting cheerfully as the headlights swept over them. Brody pulled back, blinking in the dusty white light, staring at Caitlyn like a man abruptly awakened from a dream. He saw the trickle of blood on her lower lip an instant before the truck driver shut off the headlights.

He'd hurt her. He didn't mean to, he didn't mean to.

"Carry on!" A heavy-set man climbed out of the truck and waved to Caitlyn and Brody as he walked into the bar. "Didn't mean to interrupt Mother Nature."

Caitlyn stared mutely at Brody. Suddenly she hardly recognized him, and she felt a chill whisper over her skin. He looked so distant and controlled and *closed*. "What's wrong?" she whispered. "Where did you go?"

"You're bleeding," he said. His voice was calm, perfectly normal . . . and yet not normal.

Caitlyn touched her finger to her lip. "I must have split it. It's nothing."

He didn't say anything for a moment, but he stepped back from her, his hands dropping to his sides. Still he stared at her, at those dark cinnamon eyes that were so beautiful and so clear in their trust.

"I think I could love you," he said. And then he laughed, a short, bitter sound, as if he'd just committed the biggest folly of his life.

"Brody—" Caitlyn tried to reach him, but he shook her off. She stared at him with eyes that recognized his panic but didn't understand it.

"Go back inside," he said. "This was a bad idea."

"What was a bad idea?" Caitlyn demanded, tears scratching her voice. "Coming out here? Or being able to love someone?"

Silence vibrated between them. Brody saw how much she was hurting, and it was almost more than he could bear. Slowly he lifted his hand, placing it on her cheek in silent apology. He fought the urge to take her into his arms. It took him several heartbreaking seconds before he was able to turn away, every cell in his body raw and burning.

He was halfway to his truck before he heard her say, "Don't go."

He kept on walking.

Six

___

As she paced her lonely motel room that night, Caitlyn reminded herself a dozen times that it had been Brody who'd walked away from *her*. She'd asked him to stay, but he'd kept his head up and his back straight and ignored her plea. No matter what she felt or what she wanted, she couldn't change the facts. She knew there were ghosts haunting Brody Walker, and they carried more weight with him than she did.

I think I could love you. He'd said the words, but it had been more of a startled warning to himself than a declaration. Oh, he wanted her. He wanted her as much as she wanted him, but he wasn't going to try to hold her. He simply wasn't willing to take the risk, and she didn't understand why. She felt woefully unable to understand the workings of a man's mind, especially a man who kept his feelings so rigidly protected. What had happened in his life to make him so afraid of intimacy? Was he hurting as much as she was? Or did his control extend to the point where he could choose when and if he suffered over a woman?

The last thing she did that night before finally dropping into bed was to look out the window to see if Brody's truck was parked out front. It wasn't. When the truck was still gone the next morning, the conviction that she was a wronged woman grew by leaps and bounds. He'd been out all night, doing heaven knew what with heaven knew whom. Distracting himself from his dangerous brush with sincere emotion, no doubt. Fueled by jealous fantasies, Caitlyn packed her vinyl bag and checked out of the motel, then went to the bus station and bought herself a ticket to Denver. What more auspicious place to begin a new life than the mile-high city. Besides there would be snow at Christmas and Caitlyn had always dreamed of a white Christmas. Denver would do nicely, at least for the time being.

Unfortunately her bus didn't leave until ten o'clock that night. She passed several hours wandering aimlessly through each and every shop in Moab, dragging her little overnight bag behind, her heart leaping in her chest every time she caught a glimpse of a tawny brown head.

The temperature rose to a stifling ninety-eight degrees, and she took refuge at a tiny wooden table in an air-conditioned health food store, sipping on something cold and tart called a lime smoothie. She was having trouble working up any sort of enthusiasm for the eight-hour bus trip to Denver. She felt like she was leaving the best, the brightest part of her adventure behind.

Her mind kept going back to the beginning, to her first sight of Brody with the towel knotted around his narrow waist and his hair dripping in his wild blue eyes. And she knew that long after she boarded her bus for Denver, he would still be with her. Tomorrow. The day after, the week after. She was attracted to his reckless zeal and heartbreaking good looks, but it was the need in him that touched her most. Something powerful and deep had taken hold of her, and she had no more control over it than she had over Brody himself.

She scanned the notices taped like a giant collage on the picture window, willing her mind away from Brody Walker. One brightly colored poster in particular caught her eye, bold print advertising the Canyonlands Rodeo. The Grand Entry—whatever that was—was scheduled for eight o'clock that evening. Just two short hours away.

So much for willpower.

Her thoughts were a reckless blur. Brody was riding in the Canyonlands Rodeo, which started at eight. Her bus didn't leave till ten. She could go disguised as a face in the crowd, and he would never know that she was there, watching him, drinking him in. It was a terrible, risky, wonderful idea. Just the thought of seeing him one last time sent a warm sting of fresh blood through her muscles.

One last time.

Despite the flood lights that blazed down on the outdoor coliseum, Caitlyn could still see the faint glimmer of stars blinking to life overhead. She wasn't used to seeing stars. In Las Vegas, the streets were so brightly lit they eclipsed the heavens. You walked through canyons of flashing neon, you lived in brilliant rainbows of man-made light, but you could never find the stars.

She decided she preferred the quiet lights of heaven to the electric wonderland of Las Vegas. She sat on the creaking, whitewashed wooden bleachers that surrounded the coliseum and held her face to the evening sky. It was still twenty minutes until the Grand Entry was scheduled to begin. She had come early to find just the right seat, not a reserved seat close to the arena where Brody might spot her, but far back in general admission where she was surrounded by noisy families with young children. She was dressed with the same casual conformity as most everyone else—jeans and a T-shirt, with her hair caught up at each side with red plastic combs. She felt pretty much invisible, and free to enjoy her very first rodeo. The sky was thick with twinkling lights that could be depended on to shine with or without the power company's help. The night air smelled of popcorn and beer and the distinct aroma of livestock. A crackling recording of an old western ballad was playing over the loudspeaker. Now and then someone sitting in the announcer's booth would break in and exchange a couple of jokes with the rodeo clowns cavorting in the arena. She could hear children laughing and begging for cotton candy and drinks. And crickets—she could hear crickets chirping in the cottonwood trees behind the stadium. There were no crickets on the Las Vegas strip, only the incessant jingling of slot machines.

It could have been such a perfect night, she thought wistfully. He was here somewhere, with his reckless blue eyes and that graceful, lean-hipped walk that controlled the rhythm of her heart. If only, if only...

"Howdy, ma'am."

Caitlyn nodded at the Grizzly Adams look-alike who sat down beside her. Here was another difference between the real world and Las Vegas. People said hello, and looked right into your eyes when they did it.

"It's a beautiful night," she said.

He nodded his shaggy silver head. "That it is. Not a cloud in the sky and I'm grateful for it. A rodeo isn't much fun when there's a storm blowing up around you, is it?"

"I wouldn't know. This is my first."

He frowned at her, dark brows bristling over pale blue eyes. "A girl like you, getting on in years, never been to a rodeo before? That's a damn shame, Caitlyn."

Caitlyn gave him a startled look. What a strange man. "I'm only twenty-two. There's still a little life left in—" She paused abruptly, realizing what he had just said. "How did you know my name?"

He shrugged, pulling a package of cigarettes from his shirt pocket. "Brody told me last night. I was sitting with him at the Sweet Alice bar when you came in with the Finch boys. Threw him for a loop, you did." He sighed, sticking a cigarette in the side of his mouth. "That was sweet justice, I'll tell you— finally seeing Brody Walker turning himself inside out over a woman. I've known him fifteen years, and I've watched him conquer the whole of womankind with a crook of his little finger. It's about time someone pushed his buttons."

Caitlyn opened her mouth and closed it again several times before she could shape a reply. "Who *are* you?"

He stuck out his hand, looking apologetic. "I'm a sorry old bastard—uh, coot—who never learned the social graces. Excuse my French, ma'am. Lonnie Ray Arnold, at your service. I should have introduced myself before I jumped into this conversation, shouldn't I? Well, that's the way it is with me. All breathtaking muscle and no brain."

Caitlyn couldn't help looking at the belly that hung over his big silver belt buckle. She could barely control the startled giggle that bubbled into her throat. "I see," she managed in a strangled voice. "Have you . . . have you seen Brody tonight?"

He smiled, looking like a wise old wolf. "What you mean is, has Brody seen you? No, ma'am. He's down by the chutes, helping out with the horses. No, I just happened to catch a glimpse of you sitting way up here like you wanted to blend into the scenery. I thought it might be a good time to have a word with you. I'm worried about our mutual friend."

Caitlyn sat up straight, every muscle in her body suddenly humming with tension. "Brody? Is it his ribs? Is he all right?"

"Oh, his ribs are killing him, but I'm not going to fret over that." He started chewing on the end of his cigarette like it was a toothpick. "No, it's more than that. It's you."

"Me?" she squeaked. "What do you mean, it's me?"

"Let me put it this way. Ten minutes ago, the prettiest little rodeo queen you could ever imagine wearing the tightest jeans you ever saw wiggled her way over to Brody and asked if he'd like to go dancing later on tonight. Y'know what he said to her?"

Caitlyn's fingers were suddenly damp and cold as icicles. "What?"

"He told her she had a moth stuck to her hair. Said she shouldn't use so much hair spray." Lonnie

Ray nodded, bright-eyed and completely sincere. "I witnessed this myself. The man wasn't interested. Not only that, but he wouldn't share a beer with me, he put his fist through a stall door when a horsefly bit him, and he threatened to shove my teeth through the soles of my feet when I asked him about you. He has it bad, or my name isn't Lonnie Ray. Which it isn't, actually—I was christened Lorenzo Moroni. But that's of no consequence. I speak the truth."

"What are you trying to say?" Caitlyn whispered, hardly daring to hope.

"Brody's discovered he has a heart, and he's all distraught about it. Listen, that little bugger sitting behind me just dropped half his snow cone down the back of my shirt. Why don't we take a little walk so we can talk in peace? I've got a few facts to impart to you."

Stunned, her mind working sluggishly, Caitlyn followed Lonnie Ray out of the bleachers and into the packed-dirt parking lot. There they sat on the hood of a dusty pickup truck while Lonnie Ray chewed on his cigarette and thought.

"Are you going to light that?" Caitlyn asked finally.

"Hell, no. I quit smoking five years ago and I haven't lit up since. I just do this to remember the good old days."

Caitlyn drew a shaky breath. "So you said you had something to tell me about Brody?" she asked hesitantly.

"I never learned how to beat around the bush. The boy is in love with you."

She shut her eyes for a moment. "He said that?"

"Hell, no. He's still trying to figure it out himself. Brody's a little slow when it come to risking his neck in a relationship. I don't suppose he told you about Jenny?"

"I feel like I need to sit down," Caitlyn said hoarsely.

"You already are," Lonnie Ray pointed out. "And there's no need to get all worked up, 'cause this all happened a long time ago. Jenny was Brody's wife."

Caitlyn held herself very still, afraid to move, afraid to think. Still, she felt the knife that twisted and burned deep, deep inside. Once upon a time, Brody had belonged to someone...and someone had belonged to Brody. "Brody's wife," she echoed dully. "He never told me he was married."

"Brody's not one for talking about himself. He and Jenny grew up together, childhood sweethearts and all. Hell, they were only teenagers when they got married. It didn't...well, it just didn't work out. It was a bad situation. Brody's never quite gotten over it. He's been living pretty hard since then, keeping his guard up and his expectations low."

"Why?" Caitlyn whispered. "Did he blame himself for his marriage breaking up?"

Lonnie Ray expelled a long, heavy sigh. "Well, that's the thing of it. I'd like to help that mule-brained friend of mine, but some things he's going to have to tell you himself. Till then, maybe you could just be a little patient with him. Brody's a good man underneath that lone-wolf attitude of his. A real good man." He looked up then, smiling into Caitlyn's wide brown eyes. "But I'm an interfering sort, and I think it's high time he stopped being alone. I think you'd be good for him. What do you think?"

Caitlyn slowly slid off the pickup and brushed the dirt from the seat of her jeans. Her hands were shaking badly. "I don't know what to think," she said. "What I know about men could be written on the head of a pin. I have a bus ticket to Denver in my purse and a long history of letting other people make my decisions for me. I have a terrible temper, I act before I think and I haven't made a rational decision in the past four days. How can I be good for Brody? I'm not even good for *myself.*"

"I knew it, I knew it!" Lonnie Ray chortled and slapped his thigh. "You two are perfect for each other. Damn, I'm good. I spotted it right away!"

Caitlyn stared at him for a long, perplexed moment, then turned and slowly walked to her seat in the bleachers. She watched a parade that must have been the Grand Entry. She was in a daze throughout the barrel racing and the calf roping. It was only when the bareback riding was underway that she finally came back to earth, when she heard the sound of his name echoing through the loudspeaker.

"Ladies and gentlemen, welcome a familiar face on the rodeo circuit. Give a big hand for number twelve, Brody Walker, riding Satan's Lady."

The hazy white spotlight focused on the chutes at the west end of the arena for a brief, still moment. Caitlyn stood up in slow motion, her hand pressed to her throat, her body strained and rigid. She couldn't move, she couldn't blink, not even when the huge black horse exploded out of the stall in a hurricane of sound and fury. Brody's bright blue shirt was a throbbing arc of color in the dusty scene, his tawny hair tossing and burning in the spotlight. He held one hand high in the air, and the other gripped a leather strap around the horse's neck. His body seemed to move with the same powerful motions as the wild horse, thrusting and rearing, rolling and undulating. His face was a mask of tight concentration.

"Hold on," she whispered. "Hold on, hold on...."

And then she blinked, and the entire world changed in that split second. When she opened her eyes, the horse had stumbled and was pitching forward in a wild blur of motion. His gleaming black head went down and his body rolled over Brody in a horrifying, sickening somersault. A roar of fear and excitement spread like a shock wave through the crowd, and suddenly everyone around Caitlyn was standing. She couldn't see.

She pushed her way through the crowd until she reached the stairway, then took in the scene below with glittering, agonized eyes. The horse was on its feet again, and was being herded into the chutes by two pickup men. Brody was lying motionless on his back in the dusty arena, his face the purest white she had ever seen on a human being. It was a moment that would be forever etched in her mind, a freeze-frame of heartbreak and uncertainty. She couldn't cry out. She couldn't move. She couldn't help him. She could only watch.

If he'd died and gone to hell, Brody thought, it smelled like stale popcorn and manure. And if he'd died and gone to heaven, it was a great disappointment.

He opened his eyes slowly, for all the good it did him. His vision was limited to a nauseating blur of colors and sounds, and the pain in his side was so intense he could hardly breathe. He decided it might be best to try again later, and drifted back into unconsciousness with a weary sigh.

Two minutes or two hours later, Brody opened his eyes again. He was laying on a stretcher in the back room of the concession stand. A square-built man in a paramedic's uniform was shining a penlight into his eyes.

"Give me a break," Brody said, his speech slurring heavily. "You're going to blind me."

The little light snapped off. "How are we feeling?"

"I'm peachy," Brody muttered, blinking away the sunspots that were exploding behind his eyes. "I don't know about you."

The paramedic wasn't amused. "You took quite a fall."

"I'm getting good at it." Brody tried to sit up, then gasped as a murderous pain stabbed through his side and the world careened off kilter. "Mistake," he muttered hoarsely, easing slowly down on the stretcher. "I'll just rest here a minute."

"That might be a good idea," the paramedic said matter-of-factly. "You've got a lump on your head the size of a grapefruit. I also hear you cracked a couple of ribs at another rodeo last Friday."

"I like to keep busy."

"Your fall tonight didn't help the situation. Need I say that you won't be riding in any rodeos in the near future? Those ribs of yours need a few quiet weeks to heal."

"Just wrap me in a bandage. I'll be fine."

The paramedic shook his head sadly. "She said you were going to be difficult."

Brody swallowed hard, suddenly afraid to look past the paramedic's watery blue eyes. There was only one woman in the world he could think of who would call him difficult. The woman he wished to please the most, had the world been made of wishes. "Who said I was difficult?"

"I did." Caitlyn moved from behind the paramedic and into Brody's field of vision. Her face was perfectly composed, but her eyes blazed like dark fire. "Call it an educated guess."

"Caitlyn?" Brody felt a new pain somewhere in the vicinity of his heart, as he stared at her. He'd thought she would be on her way out of town by now. He'd tried so hard to push her away. A rare and noble act, most unlike Brody Walker, but a whimsical fate seemed to be having no part of it. "What are you doing here?"

"Same as everyone else. I came to see a rodeo."

Brody was confused by the hostility she radiated. He was the injured party here. Wasn't this the part where she threw her arms around his neck and covered his face with tearful kisses? "They told me you'd checked out of the motel," he said warily. "I thought you'd left town."

"Life is full of surprises. How are you feeling?"

A small muscle ticked in Brody's jaw. "Oh, never better."

"You look terrible," she offered.

"Your sympathy is touching." He sat oh-so-slowly, dropping one leg off the side of the stretcher and resting his back against the wall. His somber blue eyes studied her as if it were the most important thing he'd ever done. "I'm beginning to feel like I should apologize for being alive."

"*No,*" she said with exaggerated dismay. "Whatever gave you that idea?"

The paramedic looked from Brody's grim expression to Caitlyn's thin-lipped composure and quickly excused himself.

"You scared him," Brody said accusingly. "What the hell is wrong with you?"

"Not a damn thing! *Pardon my French!*"

"Baby, if looks could kill, there'd be a sheet over my head right now."

Caitlyn glared at him, her lips tightening, her eyes flashing...

And then it all crumbled around her. Her head dropped and her eyes misted with tears. All the anger that had protected her poor frightened heart since she had seen Brody lying so still and helpless on the ground. The resentment that had helped her control her panic when she realized how vulnerable she had become to him, how very much she needed him. How could she have done such an absurd thing? How absolutely terrifying to realize she'd given her tender, untried heart into another's keeping and not even known it. Did everyone go through life so recklessly, or was it just the few rash souls like Brody Walker and Caitlyn Wilde?

"Can't you understand?" Her voice was low, unnaturally husky. "I watched you, Brody. I watched you fall, and I thought...when you were lying there, I thought..."

Brody gazed into the tender depths of her eyes and the last of his resistance seemed to snap inside him. He should have foreseen this moment. He should have known from the very beginning that she was the one who was going to break through all his defenses. "Look at me," he said. And when she finally lifted her head, he met her gaze with eyes that told her he understood her need and panic, because he felt it himself. "Nothing's going to happen to me, Caitlyn Wilde. Not now. Not until . . ."

"What?"

He let his gaze wander over her features, her hair. "Not until I get what I want."

"I didn't want to need you." Her voice shook.

So much was in his face: sympathy, yearning, quiet amusement. "I didn't want to need you, either."

Caitlyn's throat grew tight and peppery as she stared at the angry bruise blooming on his forehead and the smear of dirt on his cheek. All the color in his ashen face had gone to his eyes, those hungry, restless blue eyes. He had no more answers than she did. They could only stare at each other and wonder where all this would take them.

He stood up slowly, bracing his side with one hand. His legs were unsteady and his features drawn, but a flickering smile traced his lips. Answering his unspoken command, she went to him, nestling her forehead against his chest, her arms gently circling his waist. For a quiet moment they stood so, rocking together with a spiraling tenderness.

"Come home with me, Caitlyn." Brody's voice came from deep in his throat, strained and husky. "I'd like to go home."

She pulled back to look at him. "Now?"

"Now. Tonight." He held her with his eyes, his palms caressing her back. "You'd like Star Valley. It's a different world—cool and green and hidden away in the most beautiful mountains you've ever seen. We can be there by morning."

"You should rest..."

"When I'm home." Once he'd spoken the words aloud, he knew they were true. When he was safely at home, with Caitlyn by his side, he could finally rest. He could stop and breathe, and let the world spin on without him for a little while.

The house where he was born was nestled in the foothills of the Teton Mountains, surrounded by thirteen thousand acres of private land. He wanted that for himself and Caitlyn—protection, isolation, a *chance*. He wanted that more than anything in the world.

"I know it's crazy. I know I wasn't in your plans. I'm not asking for anything but...a little time. Will you give me that? Will you come with me?"

Caitlyn nodded slowly, even as she felt a resounding surprise at herself for having the courage to follow her instincts without question. She was going to do it. She was really going to do it. "Yes. If you want me."

"If I want you," he groaned, pulling her against his chest, burying his face in her neck. "Sweet girl...I want you. I want you so much, I'm not sure I'll ever be able to get close enough to you."

"You could try," she whispered hopefully.

With a shaky smile, he kissed her low on her throat. "Oh, I will. I will."

Seven

Brody drove for the first two hours. Their conversation was soft and infrequent; neither of them felt the need to talk. It was as if by mutual consent they were dwelling only on the here and now of their situation, leaving the past and the future somewhere out in the indifferent darkness. It was a sweet sort of limbo, pretending time didn't exist.

Gradually Brody began feeling the effects of his fall. His complexion paled to the color of cream cheese, and he winced and held his side whenever the truck bounced over a dip in the road. He offered a token objection when Caitlyn insisted on taking over, then immediately curled up on the seat with his head pillowed in her lap and fell asleep.

Caitlyn spread a map on the dashboard for reference, though the occasional signs on the highway assured her she was heading in the right direction. She drove past slumbering farmyards and wide-open, starlit fields, humming softly beneath her breath to stay awake. Occasionally she would hear Brody sigh, as if his dreams more than made up for his injuries. Glancing down at him, Caitlyn wished she were there, inside those dreams. When she heard him whisper her name in his sleep, she realized she was.

When the rising sun finally separated the earth from the sky, Caitlyn was amazed at the size of the mountains taking distinct shape around them. In the sleepy half-light, misty white fences gave a storybook quality to cabins and farmhouses set far back from the road. Shades and shadows of dark forest green enclosed a gentle summer world, as still and quiet as anything Caitlyn had ever known. Glancing at the tousled brown head on her lap, she felt a shiver of anticipation. This was a place where there were no distractions from the things that really mattered. The quiet yearning in her body was achingly pleasurable. The feel of this man gradually gaining a place in her heart was the sweetest, sweetest thing. He looked so boyish and innocent as he slept, yet she had seen the wildness in his blue eyes and knew the dark magic of his hands and mouth. Brody Walker was saint and sinner, boy and man, a mystery and a promise. She wasn't sure she would ever understand him, but she knew she was committed to try.

The sun was clear of the mountains and the heat in the truck was building when she pulled over to the side of the road. Brody sat up slowly, knuckling his eyes like a sleepy child. "Where are we?"

"Wyoming," Caitlyn said. "At least, I hope we are. We passed the Star Valley cheese factory a while back. I was falling asleep at the wheel, so I had to stop."

He gave her a rueful, drowsy smile. "I guess you did most of the driving. Sorry about that." He was quiet for a moment, watching her, then said softly, "Any second thoughts?"

"No." She wanted to tame his ruffled hair with her fingers, to kiss the bruise on his forehead. But he looked almost like a stranger this morning, his eyes heavy with sleep and a dark brown shadow on his square jaw. The first three buttons of his shirt had come undone, exposing his smooth, finely muscled chest. An unforgettable sensuality was reflected in his slow smile, the perceptive depths in his shaded eyes, the sleepy heat stains on his cheeks. She looked away from him and squinted out the windshield. "I hope I didn't take any wrong turns. I tried to follow the map, but I don't have much of a sense of direction."

"You did just fine. It's not far now." His hand brought her face back, and he rubbed his index finger gently under her chin. "What's happening to you?" he asked softly. "You seem so far away."

"It's not that. I was just trying..." The words didn't want to come.

"Trying what?"

"I'm trying not—" her voice broke as she swallowed hard "—not to want you quite so desperately."

Brody's eyes darkened with a new intensity. He ran his hand over her hair, just once, then pushed open his door and got out of the truck. He stood outside on the dusty shoulder of the road, eyes closed, his face raised to the sun.

Caitlyn rolled down her window. "What are you doing?"

He turned his head to look at her, his eyes as bright and blue as the summer sky behind him. His smile was on crooked. "Trying not to want you so desperately. It's not working."

Their eyes held. A car whipped past on the highway, then another, and a spasm of impatience crossed Brody's face. He stalked around the truck and climbed into the driver's side while Caitlyn slid across the seat.

"Whose bloody idea was it to drive all the way to bloody Star Valley?" he muttered softly, starting up the engine.

Caitlyn took a shaky breath and crossed her arms over her chest. "How much farther?" she asked.

"We're almost there." He stared straight ahead, the muscles in his shoulders pulsating with pure sexual tension. At the same time, a rare and unsettling tenderness welled and spilled inside him, more than he had experienced in a lifetime.

"Brody?"

"What?" The single word was soft and low.

She touched his hand on the seat between them. Immediately his fingers closed around hers in a grip that was almost painful. "We're almost there," she said softly. "You're almost home."

Brody's home was a revelation—a sprawling, five-thousand-square-foot ranch house nestled in a glorious alpine meadow. It was bordered with woods of quaking aspen and pinion pine, and strands of tall cottonwood trees lined a winding, two-mile gravel drive from the paved road.

The home had been carefully designed to create an atmosphere of permanence and tradition. Caitlyn was charmed by the chinked logs and hand-hewn beams, awed by the massive fireplace of undressed stone. She wandered through spacious rooms that were glowing with old wood and Indian artifacts in smoldering colors. Costly Navaho rugs covered stained oak flooring, serape-wrapped pillows cushioned sofas and chairs, and sun-filled windows offered picture-frame views of the shaggy green Tetons.

It was a home devoid of any obvious sumptuousness, yet breathtaking in its craftsmanship and simplicity. Dispelled was any notion Caitlyn might have had about Brody being an impoverished cowboy without roots or responsibility. This home projected a love of heritage, a respect for things that would linger in time.

Brody said little as he followed her from room to room, smiling if she smiled, frowning if she happened to fall silent.

"I've never seen anything like this," Caitlyn said quite honestly, standing in the doorway of a cozy sloped-ceilinged bedroom. "The four-poster bed... the carving is incredible."

"Billy made it," Brody said.

"Billy?"

"My little brother." He smiled faintly. "Not so little, actually. He's twenty-seven. He runs things around here when I'm gone."

Caitlyn walked over to the bed, running her palm over the puffy patchwork quilt. "And you're gone most of the time, aren't you?" she said softly. "I noticed the way you looked around when we walked in the door... like you were a visitor."

"Billy's more of a homebody than I am."

"And it's just the two of you?"

"Dad died almost ten years ago. Mom remarried and lives in Phoenix. Now it's just Billy and me and five thousand head of crossbreed Black Angus."

Caitlyn suddenly realized that her legs weren't going to support her much longer. She hadn't slept for two days, and exhaustion was sweeping over her like tides in a windstorm. She sat on the edge of the bed, slowly arching her stiff back. "Where is your brother?"

"Billy was called away unexpectedly last night," Brody replied, watching her carefully. "His big brother telephoned him from Moab and told him to spend a long weekend in Jackson Hole.''

"Did he?'' Caitlyn breathed softly. "What kind of a brother would do a thing like that?''

"A desperate brother.'' He walked slowly across the room, the sound of his boots cushioned on a bright rag rug. Standing before Caitlyn, he took her hands in his and stared down at her intently. She'd had precious little rest during the night, and it showed. Her beautiful eyes were heavy and her brow was furrowed, as if she had to concentrate to stay awake. "You've been up all night, Caitlyn. You should sleep.''

She was too tired to know what she needed...with one exception. "Hold me,'' she whispered. "I need to be close to you, Brody.''

Had she asked him to pull the sun out of the sky for her, he would have tried. He saw the look in her big tired eyes—that everything-is-moving-so-fast look—and it gave him the strength to lie down beside her on the bed, gathering her close while she sighed and curled against his chest. It was a type of loving he wasn't familiar with, but in a strange way it was more powerful than the sexual act his body was so desperate to begin. The room around him was sweet with her violet scent, soothing him, surrounding him. His body was fraught with passion, but his soul knew a curious jubilation.

He pulled his head slightly off the pillow and gazed at her. She was sleeping. Her lashes cast crescent-shaped shadows on her soft cheeks, and her hair spread in a shimmering web across her shoulders. Her mouth was sweetly parted, as trusting and defenseless as a child's. He swallowed the thick knot of emotion that pressed high in his throat, and his lips curved in a shaky smile of pure relief.

He was home.

Caitlyn woke to a hazy, unearthly glare. Dusty afternoon sunlight filled the room, slanting through the shutters on the west windows and bouncing like laser beams off glossy hardwood surfaces. She sat up slowly, blinking the sleep from her eyes. She was alone in the room, but the imprint of Brody's head was still on the pillow beside her. She touched the slight indentation and felt a gentle warmth invade parts of her that had felt cold and vulnerable for so long. She was alone in the room, but her heart drummed in her chest, knowing he was near. Soon, soon...

She stripped off her wrinkled clothes and took a hot shower, then realized she'd left her suitcase in the back of the truck. She put on jeans and a plaid shirt she found in the closet, hoping little brother Billy wouldn't mind. Her unbound breasts swayed against the light cotton of the shirt, and the too-large jeans were loosely belted around her waist, hanging onto her slight hips for dear life. She wore no underwear, no socks and no shoes, and it felt absolutely wonderful.

"A child of nature," she said proudly, standing in front of the dresser mirror as she worked a comb through her damp hair. She was exquisitely aware of her naked flesh beneath her clothing, the weight gathering and heating deep within. Deliberately she let the sensations build, unashamed and curious.

Soon.

As she walked past the bedroom window, her eyes were caught by a flash of movement outside. Brody was walking slowly through a sun-dappled grove of quaking aspen, his hands pushed deep in his pockets. His tawny head was bent, and a carpet of blue and gold wildflowers brushed his jean-clad knees. His name formed on her lips and her heart began a hard, steady escalation. He was waiting for her. She saw it in the aimless way he moved, in the impatient set of his shoulders. The very air around him seemed charged with electricity, and she felt a hard clutch of excitement.

She felt sorry for every woman in the world who wasn't Caitlyn Wilde.

She focused on physical sensation alone as she slowly walked outside. The hot sun on her face. The soft bed of grass and flowers beneath her bare feet. A languorous weight gathering in her breasts, the throb of her heartbeat all over her body. Under the circumstances, she should have felt unsure, apprehensive, but she didn't. For the first time in her life, she knew she was exactly where she belonged. What came before was forgotten. What might come next

in their lives was a mystery. This moment was everything, and she concentrated on it with a fierce intensity.

When she was but five feet from him, she stopped,
quiet and still. His back was to her. He was watching a tiny ribbon of a creek that sparkled through the
long meadow grass. A gentle breeze lifted his hair
with teasing fingers, and shades of green fluttered
and rustled softly around them.

"I'll meet you halfway," she said.

For a moment he remained stock-still, shoulders
rigid, then turned in a slow circle. Blue eyes held
brown. Brody whispered her name like a prayer, a
smile coming into his eyes like the sun burning away
the fog.

Neither of them knew who made the first move. It
didn't matter. Suddenly they came together with
enough force to knock the breath out of them, kissing wildly, tongues hungry and thrusting. Brody held
the sides of her head, his mouth slanting first one
way over hers, then another. Sunlight rained down
on them, stinging their skin, adding to the fire in
their bodies. In a heartbeat, Brody was in a state of
near agony. It had never happened this way for him
before. Somehow he knew it would never be quite
this way again.

But the woman in his arms wasn't just any woman.
He had to compose himself inside, to remember her
needs as well as assuaging his own. He broke from
her, flushed and gasping, holding her at arm's length

while his nerves screamed. To his surprise, her eyes mirrored his own—glazed and hungry.

"Don't stop," she said hoarsely. "I'm going crazy inside . . . I need you so much . . ."

"I'm trying—" he tossed back his tawny head, drawing in a hard, concussive breath "—trying to be gentle, woman."

"Don't be *gentle.*" She tugged on the front of his shirt with impatient, white-knuckled hands. "Just be . . . yourself. Show me everything you're feeling."

He pulled her close again, silent laughter lifting his chest. "Caitlyn—love, you never follow the rules. If you don't want gentleness, what do you want?"

"Honesty," she whispered. "Give me all of you. Please don't protect me. It's the last thing I need from you. I've had a lifetime of being protected. Just *take what you want.*"

His groin muscles throbbed as he imagined all the things he wanted from her. He was so hungry, so starved for her. "You're sure?"

Caitlyn smiled into his eyes, feeling both brazen and meek, sinful and glorified. "I've never liked candlelight, but I love fireworks."

They drank in each other's faces for a long, tense moment, then he slowly lifted his hand, working free the buttons on her shirt. Caitlyn shivered as the material parted, exposing her bare breasts. Her nipples hardened, feeling almost painfully sensitive to the sun. She stared at Brody, standing perfectly still as his hands found their way to her breasts. Her mouth parted on a ragged exhalation as he buried his fingers in her overly tender flesh. She wanted to groan and sigh, wanted to press against him, yet she held herself rigid with a supreme effort. Just to see, just to know how long she could balance on the knife-edge of control....

He smiled faintly, his eyes bright and knowing. Slowly he dipped his head, his mouth grazing the tip of her breast with a butterfly kiss. Caitlyn gasped, feeling the fiery nerve shocks radiate from her breasts through her muscles. Her head dropped back weakly, her fingers clutching a fistful of his shirt as she arched against him, silently begging for more. This time his mouth closed fully over her dark, sweet nipple, pulling, suckling, his tongue riding liquid fire. Caitlyn's eyes fluttered closed, her head tossing from side to side. When she thought she could stand the sweet torment no longer, he pulled back, watching as the breeze cooled and dried the wet, hardened nub, then wickedly teasing it again with his lips and teeth.

Caitlyn could hold still no longer. Suddenly she was desperate to learn more of him, as he was learning her. Impatiently she tugged his shirttail free of his pants, her palms running over his chest, his shoulders, his back. Her writhing hips found their place, rocking against the hardness between his legs. Her lips skimmed his neck, his jaw, the corner of his mouth. Brody's hand found the belt at her waist and whipped it off in one impatient motion. Caitlyn's heart tumbled into her chest as she reveled in desire, pure and simple.

Had it been like this with her? With Jenny?

The painful thought came unbidden, and she pushed it away with a furious determination. This moment with Brody was hers, and she refused to share it with anyone. She wanted only to wring every drop of joy from the moment, to forget all past and potential pain. And to give and give to this beautiful man, until he was so full of her there would never be room for anyone or anything else.

"I want to have you against me," she said, trembling fingers trying and failing to undo his shirt. "I need to feel you."

"Simplify," Brody said huskily, flashing her a bone-melting smile. He stripped off his shirt, buttons sailing. The movement hurt his injured ribs, and he winced.

"You're in pain," Caitlyn moaned distractedly.

"Oh, yes."

"Should you . . . should we . . ."

"Oh, yes." Brody flung his shirt to the ground. "Sit there."

She did as she was told, because she was a very good girl who couldn't wait to be very bad. She gave him a shaky smile and leaned back with her elbows propped in the grass. Her shirt was flying open, the waistband of her jeans bunched around her hips. "What now?" she asked huskily, her breasts thrust impudently forward.

Brody swallowed hard, staring at the picture she made. "Either I make love to you very soon or I go blind."

"I wouldn't want you to go blind," she replied, her voice deep with desire.

He smiled at her with a sexy menace. "Actually, I'm having so much fun staring at you, I kind of hate to start kissing you again."

"We can't have that," Caitlyn said softly. She held out her arms to him, the playful light fading from her eyes.

A shuddering breath fell from him as he came down to her, hands twisting into her hair as he pressed her back in their grassy bed. His thigh pressed between her legs as they rocked from side to side, his mouth slamming down on hers again and again. They kissed and thrust and ground together in a frenzy of need and began talking in breathless, disjointed words.

"Sweet..."

"Please..."

"So good..."

"Need you..."

Brody reared up suddenly, blue eyes on fire, straddling her hips as he ripped open the buttons of his jeans. Caitlyn gasped for breath, chest heaving, muscles convulsing with an exquisite, torturous anticipation. Brody kissed her once, hard, then stood up, shucking off his pants and boots with an economy of movement. Caitlyn's eyes feasted on this beautiful man who stood naked and unashamed against the bright blue sky. Her toes curled into the grass and the need suddenly became like an illness, making her weak and helpless.

"Cover me," she whispered. "Cover me with yourself. I want...I want..."

Brody stepped over her, blocking the sun. His breath caught in his throat as he took in the creamy invitation of her breasts, the soft light of surrender in her gaze.

"I know what you want," he said roughly. And then he lay down at her side, curving her into his arms. The kiss they shared was long and deep, and there was no sound but the whisper of the grass and the gentle scratching of aspen leaves overhead. Her face was soft against his callused palms, her hair spilling out in a corona around them.

Caitlyn broke from him gently, her lips shining and swollen. "Wait," she said huskily. She rose on unsteady legs and stepped out of her jeans, then let her shirt slip to the ground. He rolled over on his back, his eyes full of sexual heat as he watched her.

"I'd never dare to dream something as perfect as you," he whispered. "You are...so beautiful to me."

"Then this isn't a dream?" She came down to him slowly, her hips settling between his thighs, her arms braced on either side of his broad shoulders. Her breasts caressed his chest with a tantalizing warmth and softness. "Then it must be heaven." She lowered herself by inches, rubbing against him. "Do you think this is heaven?"

"Almost." His hands curved around her hips, pressing her into him. "We're very close, baby."

Love ran through her as she felt him swollen and hard against her, a demand, a plea. "Take me there," she begged, gathering his face into her hands for a hungry, openmouthed kiss. "Please take me."

"To heaven and back," he whispered, their mouths remaining in tantalizing contact while they slowly changed positions. He moved over her, wondering how many times he had imagined this. Imagined finding someone who would fill the lonely places in his soul, someone who would welcome him with love and laughter and sweet abandon. He poised himself above her, feeling her legs part for him. The smile on her trembling lips was a warm welcome home. And still he waited, his manhood barely brushing the part of her that was silky and moist, straining against him. "Heaven," he said hoarsely, his eyes glittering with thrilling intent.

And then he thrust down, meeting her, pressing into her as his moan of pleasure mingled with hers. Her nails dug into his shoulders, her hips rising off the ground to guide him deeper. Tears of pleasure stung her eyes and burned her throat as she held him there. Her body shuddered with a bursting sensation of desire, but it was only the beginning. Heaven help her, it was only the beginning.

He began to move inside her with a rhythm that was like nothing she had ever known. Deep, deeper... then slowly withdrawing. Another thrust, just as controlled, with the same agonizing restraint. She gasped and bit her lip until she tasted blood. She was beyond pleasure, beyond pain. He filled her, then left her aching, then filled her again. She arched her back, receiving him with all her heart, all her soul. His rhythm accelerated, and her teeth were bared as she sensed the onset of a mysterious, torturous convulsion. She was racked with anguished delight, and when she thought she could stand it no more, he took her even higher. This was both heaven and hell, and she could hardly distinguish one from another.

Her back was pressed hard to the ground, and her fevered hands were pulling up fistfuls of grass and wildflowers. She saw him like a vision above her, his eyes the same hot blue as the sky, the light of the sun in his hair, his powerful muscles straining and rippling. Her body was writhing with sheer pleasure. She whispered his name, then gasped, then cried out brokenly as her body escaped control. She was trapped, she was burning up, she knew nothing beyond wet, hot ecstasy.

From somewhere far away, she heard Brody's cry of release, but she was lost in a blinding storm of sensation. Exquisite, deep-rooted shudders gripped her muscles. One after another, coming faster and faster until she was dissolving in a shower of sparks, her spirit floating free in a haze of color and light....

She cried afterward, with joy, with love. And when he pointed out the crushed flowers she still clutched in her fists, her tears changed to laughter and she scattered them in his hair.

He hugged her tightly, closing his eyes against her hair. "Flowers and fireworks," he murmured. "I could get used to this heaven of ours."

Eight

Brody decided to cook.

They had fed the soul; it was time to nourish the body. That way, he explained to Caitlyn with boyish earnestness, they would have strength to feed the soul again.

Dressed in his jeans and beautiful bare skin, he cracked many eggs into a large pan and added whatever he could find in the refrigerator. Ham. Onions. Fresh mushrooms. He whistled while he worked, pausing occasionally to offer a besotted smile to the goddess sitting on his kitchen table.

"You're looking incredibly beautiful," he said sincerely. "The grass stains on your pants match the leaves in your hair."

"I told you I was color-coordinated." Caitlyn grinned and folded her legs beneath her, Indian-style. "Do you know, I quite like it up here. I can see more of you."

"Lucky, lucky girl," Brody mused, turning to his work. "Have I told you you're the second best thing that ever happened to me?"

"Really?" Caitlyn frowned, propping her chin on her hands. "What was the first best thing?"

He grinned at her over his shoulder. "Being blessed with my irresistible charm, of course."

Caitlyn laughed, the love inside her bubbling like a fountain. "You're a wonder, Brody Walker. Modest. Charming. Handy in the kitchen and downright masterful in a field of wildflowers. It's a shame you don't ride better. You'd be almost perfect if you could stay on a horse longer than ten seconds."

He paused in the act of chopping ham. "Bite your tongue, woman. Getting tossed off a bucking horse is a very manly thing to do. Book of John Wayne, Chapter One."

"I don't know." Caitlyn sighed wistfully, looking around the room, which glowed with shiny old wood. "If I were you, this ranch would hold more appeal for me than a mean old horse."

"A mean old horse?" Brody grabbed the handle of the frying pan and tossed the omelet in the air like a giant pancake. "Now you sound like brother Billy. Did you see how I turned that over? Damn, I'm good. Pull up a chair, ma'am. Supper is served."

As they ate, Caitlyn responded to Brody's bright-eyed exuberance with a cheerfulness she didn't quite feel. The muscles in her shoulders had tightened into knots, and she couldn't relax them. Obviously Brody didn't want to discuss his reasons for risking his neck on the rodeo circuit when he had a safe and sane life waiting for him at home. For all the fiery respon-siveness of his body, there was still a part of him that was holding back. When they had made love in the meadow, she had felt as though they were one per-son, safely nestled between what had been and what might yet be.

But now . . . now all she had of him was the faint musky scent on her body and the quiet yearning that gave her no peace. She felt they were living in a strange sort of limbo, rich with emotion yet some-how . . . precarious. She couldn't predict what would happen next. She could only take each moment as it came.

Well fed, they went to the hand-hewn porch swing to watch the sunset. Brody covered them both with a heavy Indian blanket, tucking Caitlyn's head be-neath his chin. He set the swing to rocking with his bare foot, stroking the side of her face with infinite tenderness.

"Do you know what I feel?" Brody asked softly.

Caitlyn smiled, turning her lips against his hand. "What?"

"I feel . . . quiet inside. There's no restlessness, no sense of time passing. Tomorrow won't ever come, because today is going to last forever."

Caitlyn looked at him, long and gravely. "But time *is* passing. We can't stop the sun from going down. We can't stop the leaves from turning, or the air from growing cold. It's part of life."

He took a deep breath and slowly exhaled, his eyes closing. Caitlyn could feel his resistance to reality. If things insisted on passing away, on changing, it wouldn't be with his blessing.

"I met Lonnie Ray at the rodeo," Caitlyn whispered. She laid her palm on his chest. "He told me about Jenny."

For a moment he tensed, then with a slight pressure of his hand he brought her closer to him. "What did he tell you?"

"He said the two of you were married when you were very young—and it didn't work out. That's all." Caitlyn's voice was strained as she groped for words. "Talk to me, Brody, please talk to me. I know there's something more to this, something that still hurts you. I need to know what you feel."

"What I feel," he echoed. A tight, crushing sensation sharpened in his chest. What did he feel? On the good days, he felt nothing. On the bad days . . .

His hand moved blindly in her hair. "Let it go, Caitlyn. Just let it go."

"How can I let it go? There's too much at stake, Brody." She let out her breath in a soft, frustrated sound. "I came here for no other reason than that I needed to be with you. It didn't make sense, it wasn't logical—but I'm here. Doesn't that tell you something? I've never felt for anyone what I feel for you. Can't you trust me enough to tell me about the past?"

"It's not a question of trust," Brody said. His voice was quiet, slightly hoarse. "It all happened almost fifteen years ago, Caitlyn. Why should it affect what we have today?"

"That's what I want to know," she said.

Brody didn't say anything for a moment, turning his head and staring into the sunset. "I was nineteen when I married Jenny. She was eighteen . . . and she was pregnant. Neither one of us was ready to be married, let alone be parents. But I talked her into it. You see . . . I was being noble, *heroic*. A real man lived up to his responsibilities, that's what I'd always been taught. And I intended to, I really did. I dropped out of school, got a job, did all the things a man was supposed to do." He looked at Caitlyn, giving her a faint, haunting smile. "My good intentions counted for nothing once reality set in. We started resenting each other, fighting—hell, a day never went by that we didn't fight about something. Nothing worked out the way it was supposed to."

"You were both so young . . ."

Brody dropped his head onto the back of the swing and closed his eyes. "I wish that was a good excuse . . . *I was so young*. But it isn't, not for what I did.

One night I just got sick of all the tension, the tears, the arguments...I wanted to laugh for a while, to forget the mess I had made of everything. So I left Jenny and went out to a bar with some of my old buddies from high school. We drank ourselves sick, talked about all the good times...oh, we had ourselves quite a party. I didn't get home until three in the morning." His expression changed, becoming tight and hard though his eyes remained closed. "When I got home, I found Jenny unconscious at the foot of the stairs. She ended up going into labor almost three months early. We lost the baby. A little girl."

"Oh, no...Brody..." The words were soft with a fathomless sorrow.

"She was just too small to live. The doctor said there was nothing either one of us could have done, that it was an accident. But Jenny blamed me. She said if I'd been home where I belonged, it wouldn't have happened. When she got out of the hospital, she went to her folks' house. A couple of weeks later she moved to California, and I haven't seen her since." He raised his head and looked at Caitlyn. "I made mistakes there was no way of righting. There was no going back, no doing it over. It hasn't been easy to live with."

"You can't go on blaming yourself forever, Brody."

"Can't I?" His strange smile said he knew different. "You tell me, Caitlyn...when do you stop blaming yourself for something you were responsible for? Is there a proper mourning period? I've been waiting for the day to come when I'm absolved from guilt, when I wake up and think, I've paid my dues, it's no longer my fault. But it never happens."

"You weren't responsible! You tried to take care of Jenny in the best way you knew how. It was an accident."

"It's never felt like an accident," he said tonelessly. He stroked Caitlyn's hair with an unsteady hand. Minutes passed before he spoke again. "But when I'm with you—when I'm with you, it's different. I look into your eyes and I don't feel the past anymore. All I feel is you."

Caitlyn still wasn't sure she understood his pain, but she thought she had finally glimpsed the depth of it. She pressed against him, her fingers clenching the back of his shirt. They just needed time. Given enough time, enough caring, the shadows of the past could be put to rest. "I love you, Brody," she said fiercely, her face tight against his chest. "I love you."

"Love," he whispered against her ear, as if it were a strange, exotic word he wasn't familiar with. His hands began to move beneath the blanket, seeking, demanding the comfort she offered. And then his mouth crushed hers with a startling depth of need, his tongue thrusting and possessing, desperate for full intimacy. There was a roughness in his passion, a spun-glass tension in his muscles. With their mouths mating and their bodies straining, they couldn't talk, but Brody didn't want to chance any more words. Words were imprecise tools, useless to express the emotions that churned inside him.

He threw off the blanket, urging Caitlyn to her feet, taking awkward steps toward the house while they kissed and gasped and moaned. They made it as far as the living room before they collapsed on the rug. There they shed their clothes without art, scattering shirts and jeans with careless abandon. Their final coming together was an explosion of rocketing desire, making each other wild and exhausted. Brody thrust within her as if pausing meant pain, as if time were an enemy, as if loving her was . . . everything.

They finally made it to a bed sometime during the night. Brother Billy's bed, since his room was closer to the stairs than Brody's. There they loved again, slowly and with lingering sweetness, and Caitlyn learned that soft candlelight could be just as pleasurable as flowers and fireworks.

They were curved together like spoons in the hazy light of morning when the bedroom door suddenly swung open. It was propelled with a force that sent the doorknob thudding into the wall, little chips of plaster falling like snow.

"*Whoops*," Billy Walker said. "Someone's sleeping in my bed."

Caitlyn shrieked and disappeared beneath the covers. Brody sat up slowly, shaking his head and blinking his grinning sibling into focus. "Oh, Lord, it's you. Go home."

"I am home," Billy said imperturbably. "Wouldn't you like to introduce me to your friend?"

Brody sighed and patted Caitlyn's head comfortingly beneath the sheet. "Stay right where you are, angel. I'll get rid of this crazy person."

"Crazy person!" Billy walked to the bed and sat down on the edge, nonchalantly as you please. "I like that. I spend a miserable weekend at a campground in Jackson Hole—the motels were all full up with tourists—and this is the thanks I get?"

Brody could feel Caitlyn shaking with laughter beside him. "Billy was adopted," he said, poking her hip. "He is no blood relation, I swear."

"I was not adopted!" Billy frowned at the lump that was Caitlyn. "How do you do, ma'am? I'm Billy, the good-looking one in the family. I came home just to meet you. Brody never brought anyone home before, so I knew things were serious. Can you hear me under there?"

Caitlyn lowered the sheet to her chin, wondering if her face was as red as it felt. "I can hear you perfectly," she said, looking into a pair of blue eyes just as bright, just as irreverent as Brody's. "How do you do? I'm Caitlyn Wilde."

Billy stared at her, a slow smile breaking over his face. "I do well," he said, "but not as well as Brody. You are absolutely adorable, and I'm proud to have you in my bed."

Brody buried his face in his hands. "Billy, why don't you go...somewhere? Please?"

"Why would I do that? I just returned to the bosom of my family."

"Damn it, Billy..." There was a warning note in Brody's voice.

"Then again," Billy said quickly, "you might want a bit of privacy. I understand that, I really do. I'll tell you what, bro. I don't want to make a pest of myself, so I'll just move my gear down to the little brown cabin for the time being. That way, you two can—"

"Stay away from the cabin," Brody said.

Caitlyn nearly sat up, so surprised was she by the flat, angry voice. It wasn't Brody's voice. She had never heard that cold, uncompromising tone from him. She stared at him, her expressive mouth anxious. "Brody?"

Brody didn't look at her. He continued to stare at Billy, the two brothers exchanging a silent communication.

"All right, I have a better idea." Billy suddenly jumped off the bed, his voice hearty and too loud. "You folks freshen up a bit and we'll all meet in the kitchen for lunch. Did you know it was past noon? I thought not, you wild and crazy merrymakers. You know, the living room looks like a tornado went through there, clothes scattered hither and yon...quite a sight, I'll tell you. Well, I imagine you've worked up a hearty appetite. I'll go downstairs and fix us some roast beef sandwiches, then we'll have a cozy chat. Very nice meeting you, Caitlyn. Don't bother seeing me to the door, Brody. I realize you're buck naked under that blanket and my sensibilities would be offended.''

Billy then blew a kiss to Caitlyn, eyes twinkling, and tiptoed out of the room, closing the door behind him with exaggerated care.

"What a horrible way to wake up," Brody said. "Please don't let him scare you. He's perfectly harmless."

Caitlyn emerged from the covers, pushing the hair out of her eyes. "Brody...what was that all about?"

Brody pulled her close for a cuddle. "Bad manners. Billy never learned to knock before entering a room."

She smiled faintly, but pulled back when he tried to kiss her. "I'm serious. Why did you get so angry when Billy offered to stay at the cabin?"

"I wasn't angry." His bright blue gaze remained steadily on her, warm and sustaining. "I didn't want Billy to feel like he was imposing. This is his home as well as mine."

Caitlyn relented a bit, leaning her head against his chest. "I just met him, but your brother doesn't seem like the kind of person to get his feelings hurt easily."

"You're right." Brody nibbled on her neck, his hands playing over heavenly curves. "Billy has skin like a rhino, so I won't waste any more time worrying about him. He's also frustrating, exasperating and a pain in the butt, but other than that, he's not a bad guy.''

''I like him. He reminds me of you.''

''Don't say that.'' He drew back her hair, his tongue tracing the delicate folds of her ear. ''I have more class, more tact, and I'm much better looking. You wanna fool around?''

She shivered as a new feeling of weakness came over her. ''We can't. Your brother is making us—'' a gasp here as he blew gently into her ear ''—roast beef sandwiches.''

''My brother takes a very long time when he makes sandwiches. He makes the bread first, from scratch.'' His mouth scattered warm kisses along her cheek, then hovered over her lips. ''We have all the time in the world...''

''Brody, don't.'' Caitlyn turned her head away from him, anchoring the sheet beneath her arms. ''We should get dressed.''

Brody tensed, then his arms slid from her shoulders. ''What is it?'' he asked quietly. ''Caitlyn, is it Billy? There's no need to be embarrassed. He understands.''

''Do you think so?'' She closed her eyes briefly, a bittersweet smile curving her lips. ''How could he? We don't even understand. The future's a blank page, Brody. We keep pretending that tomorrow won't ever come, but that's all it is. Pretending.''

She abruptly swung her legs off the bed, and he grabbed her to keep her from getting up. "Pretending? Was last night pretending?"

She took a deep breath, then turned her head and looked at him. In the dusty light, his tawny hair was soft and rumpled around his face. He looked heartbreakingly young and touchingly innocent, but Caitlyn knew better. This was the same man who had pulled her soul out of her body with a devastating sensual assault just hours before. Always a mystery, always a contradiction.

She pulled her legs up to her chest and dropped her forehead onto her knees. She couldn't get away from the feeling that he was holding part of himself back from her. It worried her more than she could tell him, but she forced herself to be patient. This new intimacy they shared was still too fragile to be tested by demands. "You know it wasn't," she said, the sadness in her voice muffled by the sheets. "Last night was wonderful."

He lifted her chin with his hands, turning her face toward him. His bright blue eyes were glittering with a purely sexual message that sent burning signals through her raw nerves. "We were as close as two people can be last night. I didn't think about the future, because the future didn't matter. When I'm holding you, I have everything I need in this life."

She took a shaky breath, her eyes searching his face. "There can be more, Brody. Love is more than living for today."

"How can there be more than this?" He pressed her against the pillows, kissing her with all the new-found tenderness in his soul. "This is heaven," he whispered, lifting his head. His hand slipped beneath the sheet to the mound of her femininity while he watched her eyes stretch and darken. "Don't you know that? There is nothing better to hope for or wish for. This is heaven..."

Their lovemaking was rich with passion, yet sweeter and gentler than before. There was nothing held back, nothing forbidden. Logic and doubt evaporated like steam, and there was nothing left for either of them but exquisite pleasure.

"I can't imagine what took you so long to come down here," Billy said thoughtfully, looking from Brody to Caitlyn as he munched on a carrot.

Brody bit into his sandwich, his expression pained. Caitlyn grinned behind her hand, studying the lattice pattern on the tablecloth.

"Fine," Billy said airily. "Keep your little secrets. I'm too young to be exposed to such things, anyway. Caitlyn, you haven't eaten much. Did I put too much catsup on your sandwich?"

Caitlyn had never been served a roast beef sandwich smothered with catsup before, but she didn't want to seem ungracious. "It's delicious," she said. "Really. I'm just not very hungry."

"Well, we wouldn't want it to go to waste," Billy replied, exchanging his plate for Caitlyn's. In the process, he knocked a full glass of milk off the table and into Brody's lap. He surveyed the damage with cheerful blue eyes. "Well, hell and damnation, look what I've done now!"

"Hell and damnation!" Brody shouted, his tone quite different from his brother's. He stood up, mopping his soaking jeans with a napkin. "Billy, for two cents, I'd..."

Billy immediately pulled two pennies from his pocket and slapped them on the table. "The suspense is killing me," he said cheerfully. "For two cents you'd...what?"

Brody turned a grim look on Caitlyn. "Excuse me a moment. I'm going upstairs to change my clothes and load my gun. I'll be right back."

"He's always had a short fuse," Billy said when Brody had left the room. "That's what makes him so much fun to annoy."

Caitlyn returned his boyish smile, thinking how very much he looked like Brody. "Are you two always like this?"

"You mean, deliberately trying to get each other's goat?" Billy nodded his dark curly head. "Yes, indeed. It's part of being a brother. And speaking of which, how did you happen to meet mine?"

I broke into his motel room and snuck into his bed. But I don't think we'll discuss that part. "At a rodeo," she said obscurely, crossing her fingers under the table. "He fell off his horse and knocked himself out."

"And then?" Billy pressed, unabashedly curious.

"I nursed him back to health," Caitlyn said demurely.

Billy grinned. "At least *something* good finally came out of his damned hobby. He's been trying to kill himself on the rodeo circuit for more years than I can count. I keep telling him to find a safer pastime, but do you think he'll listen to me? No way. You can't tell Brody anything—after his marriage fell apart, he just..." He broke off, looking acutely uncomfortable. "I'm sorry. I'm really sorry. Sometimes I stick my genuine alligator boot clear down to my tonsils."

"Don't be sorry." Impulsively Caitlyn touched Billy's hand on the table. "I know about Jenny."

"Well, that's a relief." Billy sighed and tipped his chair back on two legs, hooking his arms behind his neck. "I was only twelve years old when it all happened, but I still remember what it did to Brody. Man, he was a mess. It's been...hell, it's been nearly fifteen years, and he hasn't had a serious relationship since. Oh, he does a lot of talking and flirting, but it's all an act. And never, ever has he brought anyone here before." Then, as though struck by an impulse, he asked, "You do care about him? I mean...you really do care?"

Caitlyn nodded slowly, seeing the hero worship in Billy's bright blue eyes. "I care, Billy."

"Good. I'd hate to see him get hurt like that again."

Caitlyn pushed back her chair and walked to the window, crossing her arms over her chest and staring at the colors of summer. Something was nagging at the back of her mind, an unanswered question she instinctively knew was vital to her future with Brody. "Did they live here?" she asked, trying to sound casual. "Jenny and Brody?"

"No. There's another house across the creek, the little brown cabin, we call it. They lived there. It's a pretty nice place, not really a cabin at all. I've talked about moving in there a couple of times myself, actually. Believe it or not, Brody and I occasionally get on each other's nerves, and the idea of having my own place really appeals to me. But he won't hear of it. He's the only one that ever uses the cabin."

The scenery blurred before Caitlyn's unseeing eyes, her entire awareness focused on Billy's words. "You mean . . . he still stays there?"

"Now and again," Billy said evasively. "He always comes back in a hellish mood, too, so it can't be good for him. I don't understand myself why he keeps going there. Lord knows he can't have many happy memories of the place. I've told him to give himself a break and stay away from there, but he won't hear of it."

"He won't hear of what?" Brody asked, tucking a fresh shirt into his jeans as he walked into the kitchen.

Billy made a quick recovery, winking sideways at Caitlyn. "I was just telling Caitlyn how many times

I've offered to give you riding lessons so you'll stop falling off those nasty horsies." He shook his head, stood and began to clear the table. "Unfortunately you've got a head like a plank and refuse to benefit from my expertise."

Brody pulled a face and began to laugh. "Your expertise? Remember when we tried to break that sorrel mare? You cracked your head open!"

"That was you."

"It was you."

"You."

"Damn it, it was you!"

Billy grinned delightedly. "And they say the art of conversation is dead. What say we put this to the test? Down at the stable I happen to have a half-wild quarter horse I bought from Aaron Drage. How would you like to help me saddle-break her?"

Brody draped his arm over Caitlyn's shoulders. "I have a guest, Billy."

"Cluck, cluck," Billy murmured.

Caitlyn ducked under Brody's arm, spinning away from him with a brittle smile. "Don't use me as an excuse, Brody. I'll be perfectly fine on my own for a while. As a matter of fact, I'd like to take a walk, look around a little."

"Oh my, oh my." Billy looked from Caitlyn to Brody, his eyes sparkling wickedly. "Now what will you use for an excuse, brother dear?"

"All right, you're on," Brody told his brother. Then, to Caitlyn, "Why don't you come with us and witness his humiliation? It will be short and sweet, I promise."

"No," Caitlyn said quickly, too quickly. "You two go ahead. I'll enjoy a nice long walk. It's a beautiful day."

Naturally the quarter-horse challenge took precedence over the lunch dishes. Brody and Billy left immediately, squabbling companionably and slamming the screen door behind them.

Caitlyn sank down on a chair, feeling as if she had been caught in a whirlwind. Her heart was lodged painfully in her throat and her stomach was knotting. She hunched forward, as if preparing herself for some invisible blow.

Why would Brody insist on going back again and again to a home that by all accounts had seen more tears within its walls than laughter? Why would he react so violently to the thought of Billy living there, keeping the cabin to himself like a jealous lover?

Caitlyn closed her eyes, pressing her fist to her mouth. Perhaps he wasn't haunted by the past, after all. Perhaps Brody was the one doing the haunting, stubbornly lingering in the shadows of a time gone by. He talked of love and passion and satisfaction, but always shied away from discussing the future with her. The answer could be so simple, so terribly simple. He could never reach out for the future while he was clinging so hard to the past.

What was it he had said to her? *I've been waiting for the day to come when I'm absolved from guilt....* *But it never happens.*

What if it never did?

She had no idea how long she sat there, staring at nothing. There were so many things to think about, and she had to be sure that she was right. This was too important to her to make a mistake, to read him wrong. She needed the truth before she made any decisions. She had wanted a chance to tackle life head-on, willy-nilly, and here it was. She had already experienced the joy. She had no choice now but to take the pain along with it.

She stood up, her stomach compressed into a hard, burning knot as she walked to the door. There was something she had to do, and she had to do it now, without drawn-out agony or hesitation. She needed to see the house where Brody had once lived with the woman named Jenny. Somehow she knew if there was any truth to be found, she would find it there.

Nine

Caitlyn crossed the cobblestone bridge over the creek, then followed a marked path through a wood of quaking aspen. The trail had been well cared for, she noted with a sinking heart. She would have felt so much better had it been overgrown and lost in weeds.

Perhaps half a mile from the main house, the trees dwindled away and opened up to a sloping green lawn. Atop a small hill sat a charming log home, surrounded by a deep covered porch. Caitlyn realized she was approaching the house from the back. There was an irrigation ditch between the lawn and lush green strawberry beds, a rainbird attached to a long strip of green hose and white lawn furniture set beneath a heavily crowned shade tree. The house had a lonely look to it, empty but not neglected. Caitlyn walked slowly around to the front, where she saw a long asphalt driveway leading to the main road. Her eye was caught by the faded tole painting on the white mailbox: *The Walkers*.

Swallowing hard, she tried the front door. To her surprise, it was open. She walked inside, the hazy glow of sunlight behind drawn curtains lending the house a dreamy, unreal quality. She gave herself a minute while her eyes adjusted to the shadows.

One by one, the furnishings took shape: a casual, red and white checked sofa in the living room, a braided rag rug with all the colors of the rainbow, a cupboard filled with a few pieces of good china and the inexpensive sort of knickknacks that newlyweds would have. A hanging plant in the window looked green and healthy. Caitlyn walked over to it and touched the soil, finding it damp. She imagined Brody keeping things up around here, doing what he could to keep the past alive, and a soft heat of anger filled her chest.

The kitchen was small, but decorated with bright country colors that made it seem larger. There was a wooden trestle table near a bay window, topped with a vase of plastic flowers. A half-used roll of paper towels hung beneath the cabinets, and mushroom-shaped magnets dotted the refrigerator. Caitlyn picked up the telephone receiver from the wall and listened to the dial tone, then replaced it with stiff fingers. Damn the man—he hadn't lived here for fifteen years, but he couldn't bring himself to disconnect the telephone service.

But the worst was still to come. She walked upstairs to the bedrooms, pausing at the first open door. It had been decorated as a nursery, with circus-print vinyl wallpaper and a white crib. A Mickey Mouse mobile was attached to the headboard, still and motionless in the heavy air.

Caitlyn had seen enough. She tore down the stairs and ran out the door, her anger burning so hot she could hardly breathe. Half-running over the path to the main house, she was propelled by fury, fear and frustration. How could Brody have done this to himself all these years? So much life, wasted. So much pain, self-inflicted by a man who would rather face the past over and over than try and make the future work.

Brody and Billy were in the kitchen when she returned, both dusty and sweaty, tossing down giant-size glasses of water.

"The horse won," Brody said, giving Caitlyn a welcoming smile. His blue eyes seemed to burn like lasers in his flushed face. "How was your walk?"

"Billy, will you excuse us for a minute?" Caitlyn said, never taking her eyes from Brody's face.

Billy set his glass on the counter, looking from his brother to Caitlyn. "I was just going…somewhere," he said. "I do that quite a bit, lately."

Brody watched Billy practically sprint out the back door, then turned to Caitlyn with a frown. "If you could see the look on your face right now," he said slowly, "you'd know why Billy was moving so fast. What's wrong?"

"The scenery is breathtaking around here," Caitlyn said. Her words were low and scornful, and the raw color in her cheeks was born of heartbreak. "Especially the little house I visited on the other side of the creek. It took my breath away, Brody, it truly did."

Brody stared at her, feeling like something was breaking apart inside him. "Why did you go there?"

"I wanted to pay my respects," she shot back, dark eyes flashing. "That's what you do when *you* go there, isn't it? Correct me if I'm wrong, but isn't that some sort of a shrine?"

He took a deep breath, but for the life of him he could think of nothing to say. This was a woman he had never seen before, a fiery she-cat disguised as a petite ball of fluff.

"What's the matter?" she asked in a silky voice. "Cat got your tongue?"

"This conversation is getting us nowhere. I won't fight with you." Brody tried to take her in his arms, hoping to distract this unnerving little woman, but she pulled away with a snarl.

"No! Not this time, you don't. Love is more than sharing bodies. It goes deeper than that. It's strong and it's comforting and it's wonderful, because it helps you make it through this unpredictable life. But you know what, Brody? You can't love someone else unless you love yourself first. And you, my dear friend, are a miserable number-one failure at loving yourself!''

Brody's emotions collapsed to a flat, nerve-racking blank, like the high pitch of the emergency signal on a radio station. ''I don't need this,'' he muttered, trying to turn away. ''I don't know what the hell has gotten into you, but you're sure ruining a damn fine afternoon.''

Caitlyn's hand shot out, closing around his arm in an incredibly bruising grip. She loved him and she hated him, and she wished she was big enough to shake him until his teeth rattled. ''That's the difference between you and me, Brody. I'm willing to face the facts. I'm willing to ruin a damn fine afternoon. And I'm willing to lose you rather than share you with your dead past.''

He tried to pull away, but her fingernails dug into his skin. ''You're overreacting. You don't know what the hell you're talking about.''

''You're a martyr, Brody. You live the part with charm and you live it with style, but you're nothing but a martyr. You want me, but you don't want me bad enough to take a chance again. It's ironic, really. In the past few days, you've helped me to believe in myself, to honestly *like* myself. That's a lesson you've never been able to learn.'' Abruptly she let go of his arm and took a step back. "I can't think of any reason I should stick around here, can you?"

Brody stared at her, feeling as though he were on the other side of a plate glass window, like he could only catch scraps of her words and meaning. "What are you trying to tell me? You want to leave?"

"I never learned to share, remember?" She turned on her heel, blinking furiously at the tears burning her eyes. "You'll never make an emotional commitment to me, Brody. You're already committed to the past. I deserve better than second best."

Brody watched her walk out of the room. He was choking on a knot of fury in his throat. Who the hell did she think she was? She didn't know a damn thing about the demons that drove him, his fears, his insecurities.

Because you never told her.

But Brody was in no mood to listen to the voice of reason, not when he was cornered and hurting so badly he could hardly breathe. Panic was in him, everywhere. A white-hot rush of adrenaline sent him bounding up the stairs to Billy's bedroom. Caitlyn was throwing things into her ridiculous striped duffel bag, breasts heaving, a furious look of determination on her face.

"So that's it?" he ground out, his hands braced on either side of the doorway as if to block her exit, shoulders bulging with tension. "You're picking up your toys and going home?"

"No, I'm not going home. Unlike you, I know what I want. I'm going to Denver, like I planned. I've discovered I'm a pretty resilient girl when the chips are down. I'm going to be just fine."

"Well, bully for you," Brody said, infuriated by her coldness, her independence. "Happy trails."

She lifted her head, staring him down with dark woman eyes that saw too much. "Amazing. You won't even put up a token fight, will you, Brody? You're so afraid of failing again, you won't even try."

"Would it do any good? You're a big girl. You know what you want."

"That's right," she whispered fiercely, zipping up her bag. "And I'm not going to find it here."

Brody followed her down the hall and stood at the top of the landing as she took the stairs two at a time, her bag bouncing one step behind. "Has it occurred to you that you may have a transportation problem?"

She didn't pause, didn't turn. "I still have the keys to the truck."

"What, you're stealing my truck now?"

"Have Billy give you a lift into Jackson Hole. You can pick it up at the bus station. I'll leave the keys under the seat."

"Damn it, Caitlyn, you can't just walk out like this!"

She stopped at the front door, her fingers on the knob. She looked at him over her shoulder, her reflective gaze lifting to his. "Why?" she said flatly. "What do you have to offer me?"

Silence fell heavily between them. Brody's heart began a slow pounding in his chest. "Maybe you're right," he said hoarsely. "Maybe you do deserve better."

She shook her head, tears overflowing. "You stupid, stupid man. We could have had it all."

Just then the knob turned beneath her hand. Billy poked his head around the door, taking in the emotionally charged scene with wide blue eyes.

"Oh, Lord," he said.

"Excuse me, Billy." Caitlyn pushed past him and ran down the front steps. She tossed her bag onto the back of the truck, then walked around and got in. Billy came bounding out of the house just as she turned the keys in the ignition.

"What the hell happened?" He raised his voice to carry over the sound of the gears grinding as Caitlyn shifted into reverse. "Where are you going?"

"Jackson Hole."

"Why?"

"Ask Brody." The tears were coming freely now, dripping off her chin, running in her mouth. "I'm sorry, Billy. I can't force him to let go of the past. No one can."

Billy stood on the driveway until the pickup was out of sight. Then he turned, looking at the house with a tight-lipped expression.

"You son of a bitch," he said. "You stupid son of a bitch."

The house was empty without her.

Brody went upstairs to his room and sat on the edge of his bed. He tried to think, but nothing would come. The emptiness was in the air around him, making him cold. He looked at his hands and saw they were shaking.

It was then he realized a not-so-subtle change had taken place inside him. For the first time in years, he was more afraid of the future than he was of the past. He imagined waking day after day, missing her, needing her so. He swallowed hard, the passage of air in his desert-dry throat agonizing. He saw her in his mind—her soft doe eyes, that evocative child's mouth, the hint of rose in her smooth cheeks. Sweet, innocent, lovely you, he thought; soiled, cynical me.

A lucky escape for the heroine of the tale. She saved herself, which was a damn good thing, considering the hero's tendency to fall down on the job.

Suddenly he had to move, to expend some of the energy that was crackling along his nerve endings like winter frost. He ran downstairs and out the front door, then around the back of the house to the woodpile. He stripped off his shirt and picked up the ax, attacking the dry logs with furious intensity. Again and again he swung the ax, gradually giving his mind and his body to the age-old rhythm of physical work. Steel whistled through air and into wood, and the impact shuddered through his arms, his shoulders, his back. His injured ribs burned like fire, but he repeated the powerful motions in a mindless cadence until his bare skin shimmered with perspiration and a slow nausea bunched in his stomach. He took one final bone-jarring swing, teeth bared, and buried the ax head deep in the chopping stump. It was all he could do to pick up his shirt and walk into the house without collapsing.

Billy met him in the front hall. Brody's shirt was hanging outside his pants, and high spots of color burned on his cheeks. "You look like hell," Billy said. "What did you do, try to run after the truck? No, no...you wouldn't do that. Too much effort required."

"Get out of my way."

But Billy moved forward, standing chest to chest with his brother. "I don't think so. We're going to have a talk, me and you."

Brody smelled whiskey on his brother's breath. He looked in the living room and saw a half-empty bottle on the oak bar. "Why the hell are *you* drinking?" he demanded, as if he had far more reason to drown his sorrows in alcohol than his brother.

"Because I'm related to an ass," Brody replied, bright-eyed and quite sincere. "Besides, I'm not drunk. I'm just very courageous. Whiskey always makes me brave, and I need to be brave right now."

"Why?" Brody muttered, rubbing his sore shoulder.

"Because I'm going to do this."

Billy was two inches shorter and ten pounds lighter than his brother, but he swung his fist into Brody's jaw with enough force to send Brody staggering. He hit the wall and stared at Billy with shocked eyes, then raised the back of his hand to his lip and found blood.

"What the hell did you do that for?" Brody shouted, righting himself on two wobbly legs.

"Because it was called for," Billy answered, both fists at the ready. "Because you are a stupid son of a bitch. Because this afternoon you let the best thing that has ever happened to you walk out that door." Then, when Brody just stared at him, "What? You won't even fight when someone hits you first? Are you a coward *and* a stupid son of a bitch?"

"I'm not going to fight you! You're my brother, damn it!"

"I can't help that! Nobody asked me if I wanted a lily-livered chicken heart for my only brother. What's the matter with you, Brody? Don't you know how to go after something you need? Don't just stand there, *fight* me!" With a frustrated snarl, he drove into Brody, burying his head in his stomach and sending them both flying to the ground. An antique coat-rack tipped and fell, catching a huge beveled mirror on the wall and sending it crashing to the floor in a shower of glass.

"My ribs," Brody said hoarsely. "Hell, that hurt. Get off me, Billy, you idiot... I can't breathe."

Billy got slowly to his feet, his boots crunching on the shattered glass. He stared at his brother for the longest time, then muttered a soft oath and helped him up.

"So are we through now?" Brody gasped, looking at his brother warily. "Or are you going to go crazy again?"

"I forgot about your ribs," Billy said. "That doesn't make it a fair fight."

"Yeah, well, you're drunk. That makes us even... *if* I was going to fight you, which I'm not."

"I'm not drunk, I'm—"

"Courageous," Brody sighed. "I know." He walked slowly to the stairs and sat on the bottom step. After a moment, Billy joined him.

"I'm right, you know," Billy said presently. "She *was* the best thing that ever happened to you."

"I know," Brody admitted softly.

"So how can you justify letting her walk out of your life?"

"I don't know."

"Well, fine. This has been a very productive conversation." Billy stood up, a greenish tinge to his complexion. "I have to go upstairs and be sick now, but first I want to point something out. You've been punishing yourself for being human for an awfully long time now. It's all real noble of you, but... hell, wouldn't you rather be happy?"

Brody sat on the stairs long after Billy had gone. He sat with his arms on his knees and his head bowed, asking himself over and over again if it could possibly be as simple as Billy had said. *Wouldn't you rather be happy?* He felt as if a great clutter of debris was stirring and shifting inside him, making room for a breath of clean, fresh air. He was so tired of carrying the weight of the past around on his shoulders. Until he solved it, until he somehow made amends for it, he'd thought he had no choice, but what if he'd been wrong? What if he simply had to let it go?

He sat up a bit straighter, because his ribs were killing him, but his mind was racing, racing through the past. A spasm of pain shuddered through him as he thought of the mistakes, the consequences, and then the pain eased as he willed himself to let it go. He was only a man, woefully human, yet the most beautiful, the most precious woman in the world had seen something in that woeful human to love. Surely that counted for something? And if she was willing to take this extraordinary risk for him, shouldn't he be willing to risk anything and everything for her?

And then Brody was standing, and the smile that tucked his blue eyes and lifted his lips came straight from his heart. To hell with protecting himself, always standing on the sidelines, always holding back. The oppressively heavy load he had carried around so long was gone, and in its place a fine new courage sang through his veins. Buoyed by this sensation of permanent change, he made a heroic decision.

He wasn't going to let the best thing that ever happened to him get away.

Ten

Caitlyn made it to Jackson Hole with no trouble. She was getting very good at driving a truck, very good at reading a road map, very good at lifting her chin bravely and forging ahead. She went to the bus station to wait for her bus. She was utterly and completely miserable, but that was to be expected. She would survive. Like anyone else, she was capable of making great, catastrophic mistakes—such as falling in love with Brody Walker—and she was capable of surviving and learning from those mistakes. In her heart she had a greater understanding of the frailties and the resilience of her own nature. This was what she had wanted from the beginning, the freedom to become herself, warts and all. It was a bittersweet victory, since she had also learned more about heartache than she would have liked. She mourned her lost love with every breath, but she regretted nothing. She had discovered a wonderful strength within herself, and she knew she was equal to any challenge. She had unfettered herself, no matter how painfully, from a relationship that could only cause her heartache. If she could do that, she could do anything. Yes, she loved Brody Walker as she had never loved another man. But she also loved herself, broken heart and all.

There were still two hours before her bus left, and she had a few important things to do. She spent sixty dollars on a bright yellow tube dress that dipped low at the neck and molded her hips with tender loving care. In the dressing room at the department store she brushed out her long auburn hair until it danced down her back like a bright butterfly. She pinched her cheeks until they glowed, then stood in front of the mirror and smiled with faint satisfaction. If Brody could have seen her looking like this, it would have driven him crazy.

She had a fine meal in a fine restaurant, not giving a second thought to the money she was spending. Part of loving yourself was pampering yourself when you needed it the most. She asked for a telephone and placed a long distance call to Nicky. After his initial outburst he calmed down quite a bit, even managed a faint laugh when she told her she was excited about taking her second bus ride.

"And I want you to come to dinner in two weeks," she said. "I've missed you."

"Dinner? Where?"

"I don't know," Caitlyn said peaceably. "But I'll let you know. I can promise you there will be fresh flowers on the table and most interesting conversation."

"Caitlyn, at least let me send you enough money to—"

"Absolutely not," she said, her tone brooking no argument. "I'm going to have a job by then. Don't ask me what job, I don't know. I have a college degree in fine art, so I certainly should be able to do something. Sooner or later I'll find my niche, Nicky. Right now I'm more concerned with enjoying the journey than reaching the destination."

There was a long silence. "You've changed, Cat."

"I hope so," Caitlyn said softly. "Take care, Nicky. I'll call you soon."

As she walked out of the restaurant, Caitlyn was pleasantly aware of the admiring glances she received. She felt quite beautiful, if brokenhearted. She told herself fiercely that today was a fresh beginning, that there would be no looking back. She wasn't the kind of person who could be satisfied with half of anything. Brody had offered the shadow of love, but not the substance.

You told me once you'd meet me halfway, Brody. But you never did, you never did.

With another half hour to kill, she went to the bus station and bought a magazine to read. There were quite a few people milling around, some tourist types and a couple of talkative servicemen who dogged her heels from the bench to the coffee machine to the picture window and back again. Caitlyn tried to be sociable, but she finally hid behind a magazine, reading a timely and informative article entitled, "Men! What's to Love?" When the call for boarding was announced, she quickly gathered her things and tried to slip past the boys in uniform, but to no avail. They blocked her path, begging for the opportunity to carry her bag. She gave them a sassy grin that felt like plastic on her face and told them she was a big girl and could carry it herself.

At that moment, the glass door swung open and a broad-shouldered man walked in. Caitlyn looked up absently, then she uttered an involuntary sound between a squeak and a whimper and felt herself backstep. Brody. Brody, Brody...

He found her and pinned her against the wall with those bright blue eyes. His smile came slowly, spreading and stretching to a full-fledged grin. A crooked grin, Caitlyn noticed with some confusion. His lower lip was swollen, and a shiny new, fire-engine-red bruise bloomed on his jaw.

He walked toward her slowly, the sound of his cowboy boots unnaturally loud on the wooden floor. Hips rolling with a confident masculine rhythm, shoulders broad and sweetly muscled beneath a blue denim shirt. Fever colors shadowed his cheekbones, the colors of excitement, of intensity.

Caitlyn didn't realize she was walking backward, away from him, until she came up hard against the wall. Her bag slipped from her nerveless fingers and hit the floor with a thud.

He said, "I love you."

Caitlyn closed her eyes, palms spread flat on the cold cinder-block wall on either side of her hips. She managed to utter one word: "No!"

His hands closed over her shoulders, his fingers gently stroking the ridge of her collarbone. "I love you."

She tried to melt into the wall, desperate to escape the coaxing presence of his thighs against hers. In the private world behind her closed eyes, she felt a spinning, dizzying sense of upheaval. What sort of cruel game was he playing? "Go away, Brody. Go away, or I'll...I'll—"

"You'll what, sweetheart?" His tone was kind, even helpful.

She opened her eyes, her numbed gaze wandering over his shoulder to the arrested expressions of the two young servicemen. "I'll sic *them* on you," she whispered fiercely, nodding at them.

Brody looked over his shoulder for a moment, then turned to Caitlyn, so much love and laughter in his gaze she felt her heart turn over. "So be it," he said. "Before I came here, I realized I was willing to fight an army for you. Technically they're Navy, but the principle is the same. I will challenge the world for you, madam. I will go down on my knees, I will wear my bleeding heart on my sleeve, I will follow you to the ends of the earth, if need be. No mountain is too high, no ocean too wide. I love you to the height and depth my soul can reach. If you leave me, this earth will be a tomb.''

''You're crazy!'' Caitlyn stared at him, aghast. This wasn't Brody. This was an alien being who had inhabited Brody's body. ''Are you drunk? Did you have an accident? Did you fall off another horse and hit your head?''

''I'm not crazy,'' Brody replied, with equal amounts of amusement and indignation. ''I'm romantic. I'm laying my heart at your beautiful feet.'' Then, as an afterthought, ''I did have a little fight with Billy, but I didn't hit my head. Believe it or not, the boy managed to knock some sense into me. I realized something amazing. Brody Walker is the hero of this tale. Better late than never, I've come to rescue you.''

''Excuse me.'' One of the Navy boys tapped Brody on the shoulder. ''It seems to me you're annoying this lady.''

Smiling, Brody held Caitlyn's eyes, his own delivering a tidy little message. *It's up to you. I am prepared to do battle.*

''He's not bothering me,'' she managed through a tightly constricted throat. ''We're...friends. Thank you very much for your concern.''

Her would-be rescuer still looked suspicious. "The bus is boarding now."

Caitlyn nodded. "I'll be right there."

"I beg to differ, ma'am," Brody said in his best cowboy drawl. "You're coming with me. We're going to get married and have a passel of young 'uns."

"Oh, dear heaven." Caitlyn couldn't take this any more...the curious, amused stares from the people in the waiting room, the low growling noises from the military, Brody's mind-boggling behavior. She kicked Brody in the shin and ducked under his arm, then ran out the door with her hair tossing in a fiery wave.

Brody stared after her, a satisfied smile on his face. Yes, indeed. It was going very well. You could have knocked him over with a feather when he'd walked into the bus station and seen her in that bright yellow dress. He didn't know quite what he had expected, but it hadn't been a copper-haired beauty poured into something that looked like lingerie. Now that he thought about it, though, it was just the sort of thing Caitlyn would do under the circumstances. What a woman. What a remarkable, glorious woman.

Still smiling, he picked up her little vinyl bag and walked out the door.

She found a phone booth around the corner, just out of reach of the light from the street lamp. She didn't want to make a call. She wanted to hide like a sniveling coward until the world righted itself again and logical thought returned. Her heart was pounding, her hands were shaking, and her flesh was prickling. It wasn't fair. Leaving him had been so hard, so incredibly painful, and now he was here spouting love words and laying his heart at her beautiful feet? *A passel of young 'uns?* Who did he think he was, anyway? John Wayne?

A tall, dark shadow slowly approached the booth. Caitlyn stopped breathing, planting both feet against the hinged door to prevent it from opening.

Brody raised his fist and knocked gently.

"You can't do this to me," Caitlyn cried, pointing at him with a shaking finger. "I'm not a toy to play with when it suits you."

Brody could hear her, but only barely. He stepped closer, pressing his palms against the glass. Then he smiled and mouthed the words: "Let me in."

"I can't." She shook her head, her vision blurring. "You let me go, Brody. You didn't even try to stop me."

"I know I hurt you," Brody said, raising his voice to carry through the glass. The few late-night tourists strolling by could also hear him, but he wasn't concerned with them. "I'm sorry. I swear I'll spend the rest of my life making it up to you. I love you, Caitlyn. I would do anything for you, risk anything for you, become anything for you. I would, my love, I swear I would."

She sank weakly against the glass, her dark eyes shimmering with panic, with anxiety and finally...with hope. "You love me," she whispered.

He couldn't hear her, but he read her lips. His smile was soft, breathtaking in its sweetness and sincerity. Slowly, holding her eyes, with God and half a dozen tourists as witnesses, he went down on his knees. It was a romantic and heroic gesture that came deep from within his captive heart, from his grateful soul.

Caitlyn started to cry and opened the door.

They shared a doughnut and a cup of coffee at an all-night café. They sat at a secluded corner table and spoke of the future, which was rich with possibilities, and never gave a thought to the past. So absorbed were they in one another and the miracle they had been granted, they didn't notice the black Jaguar pulling up to the curb outside. It was the merest coincidence that Brody happened to tear his eyes away from his love long enough to notice the portly, dark-haired fellow who trudged through the door. He looked tired, frustrated and hungry.

"Look there," Brody whispered, squeezing Caitlyn's hand and nodding toward the new arrival.

Caitlyn's mouth tipped in a wide grin as she recognized Lyle Switzer waiting for the hostess to seat him. "The poor man," she said. "He's still looking for me."

"He has terrible instincts," Brody said, shaking his head. "He's always two steps behind us and never knows it."

"We should tell him the search has been called off."

"We should."

They sat quietly for a moment. Caitlyn looked over her shoulder, humming softly under her breath. There was an emergency exit door not three feet away, partially screened by a huge potted plant. "Where do you think that door leads?" she asked casually.

They stared at each other, identical smiles blossoming. Brody pulled a ten dollar bill out of his wallet and put it on the table. He stood up, holding out his hand. "Let's find out."

* * * * *

SILHOUETTE·INTIMATE·MOMENTS®

IT'S TIME TO MEET
THE MARSHALLS!

In 1986, bestselling author Kristin James wrote A VERY SPECIAL FAVOR for the Silhouette Intimate Moments line. Hero Adam Marshall quickly became a reader favorite, and ever since then, readers have been asking for the stories of his two brothers, Tag and James. At last your prayers have been answered!

In August, look for THE LETTER OF THE LAW (IM #393), James Marshall's story. If you missed youngest brother Tag's story, SALT OF THE EARTH (IM #385), you can order it by following the directions below. And, as our very special favor to you, we'll be reprinting A VERY SPECIAL FAVOR this September. Look for it in special displays wherever you buy books.

 *Silhouette Books*®

Take 4 bestselling love stories FREE

Plus get a FREE surprise gift!

Coming Soon

Fashion A Whole New You. Win a sensual adventurous trip for two to Hawaii via American Airlines®, a brand-new Ford Explorer 4 × 4 and a $2,000 Fashion Allowance.

Plus, special free gifts* are yours to Fashion A Whole New You.

From September through November, you can take part in this exciting opportunity from Silhouette.

Watch for details in September.

* with proofs-of-purchase, plus postage and handling